THE LIVES OF A *CORRUPT FAMILY*

LISA BROWNING

Zeta Publishing
Ocala, FL

Zeta Publishing, Inc
3850 SE 58th Ave
Ocala, FL 34480
www.zetapublishing.com

Ordering Information:
Quantity sales. Special discounts are available on quantity purchases by corporations, associations, and others. For details, contact the publisher at the address above.
Orders by U.S. trade bookstores and wholesalers. Please contact
Zeta Publishing: Tel: (352) 694-2553; Fax: (352) 694-1791 or visit
www.zetapublishing.com

ISBN: 978-1-947191-50-1 (sc)

ISBN: 978-1-947191-51-8 (e)

Library of Congress Control Number: 2017957528

Printed in the United States of America

This book is dedicated to my wonderful husband who has showed me that not everyone is a bad seed and for his patience while helping me through many tough times in my life as well as assisting me with the writing of this book.

Contents

Introduction

This book describes the interactions and lives of a family living in the latter part of the twentieth century and early beginnings of the twenty-first century America. The setting is within the eastern states of Ohio, West Virginia and North Carolina. It provides a true picture of various situations where love and forgiveness have been replaced with anger, resentfulness and hatred. In order to avoid embarrassment, the names of various family members have been changed.

Chapter One
Betrayed

As far back as I can remember, I had a really great childhood. At least the first half of it was great. Mom and dad had seven children. I was the fifth in the order of their birth. Mother Sheila and father Keith had known each other for their entire lives. They knew each other during their childhood and they always played together. It was in 1975, when mom was seventeen and dad was nineteen that they learned they were pregnant with their first child, my sister Cindy.

Cindy was born in December of the same year. After Cindy was born mom and dad just could not get along. Soon afterwards, they separated and dad went back to West Virginia while mom stayed in Columbus, Ohio.

While in Ohio mom met a man named James Stamo. He and mom got married after a few short months of dating. Since having Cindy, she would allow my father to visit with her. Soon after her marriage to James, mom discovered she was pregnant with her second child. When mom told James they were going to have a baby they began having marital problems and soon thereafter they split up.

Dad still loved mom and Cindy so much that they got back together and he also loved the baby my mother was carrying. In March of 1977 mom gave birth to my sister Maranda. Dad was at the hospital when Maranda was born and gave Maranda his last name. At this point in time my father and mother were not married as my mother was still in the process of getting a divorce from James Stamo, Maranda's biological father. Mom and dad stayed together until they began to have trouble again at which time they separated once again.

After their second break-up mom met a man named Robert Ralph. Soon after meeting him, she became pregnant with her third child and in the late spring of 1979 my sister Vivian was born. Later, while dad was visiting with mom, Cindy, Maranda, and Vivian, she learned she was pregnant again with her fourth child. When Robert discovered she was pregnant, he and my mother separated. This is when my dad, told my mom that he wanted her and all the children.

When mom delivered my brother Bradly in April of 1980 my dad was there. Things started looking better for the family as my father loved mom and each of the children even though some were not his biological children. By the summer of 1981, I was born into the world at 1:31 AM on June the 10th. Then, in November of 1982, Keith David, Jr. was born. Then, two years later, in March of 1984, sister Tabitha was born. After having seven children, mom and dad decided there should be no more children so mom had her tubes tied. This, no doubt, made my daddy very happy.

By October of 1985 mom and dad were finally married. It was my father's first marriage and my mom's second. In December of 1985 Vivian and Bradly's biological father, Robert Ralph, passed away. I cannot ever remember him having visited my sister Vivian or brother Bradly. By the early 1990's mom and dad began having disagreements like anyone else. They drank a lot and every Friday mom would have drinking parties with some of the local neighborhood drinkers. Mom would play old loud country music while we children would stay out of site. Sometimes my mother and father's parties would go fine and everything would be fun. Other times the parties would turn into yelling, fighting, and screaming with the police getting called. I remember my mother always teaching us seven children to go to our bedrooms and hide because when my father drank beer he would sometime become very mean.

One day, in the middle of my parent's many disagreements, my siblings and I witnessed something very horrible. Mom was, for some reason unknown to us, very upset with my father for whatever reason. Dad had gone to work this day. He had a beagle puppy that he adored. The pup, which had not yet been potty trained, went into the living room where it soiled the carpet.

Mom took a broom, she unscrewed its handle, and proceeded to beat the pup with the broom stick. She beat it unmercifully while all the time we children watched in horror. When she finally stopped beating it, it was barely alive. She threatened us kids and we were ordered not to say anything to dad. Otherwise, mom would beat us. When dad got home from work that evening, the dog was lying on the floor in a corner of the dining room. Mom told some story to my father that the dog had somehow gotten out of the fenced yard. She told dad that she ran outside into the street to pick up the dog as it lay there. She told him a man in a truck had hit the dog. This caused dad to go looking for an invisible man that of course he could never find.

He took the pup to the local animal hospital. The pup had several cuts and broken bones. It was living but not moving. We were told that if it did live it would be paralyzed could never be able to walk again. As a result, dad had it put to sleep. Mom thought she had gotten away with the perfect crime.

But, not so, a few days passed when Tabitha spoke to dad about how she missed the dog. Tabitha was about six or seven years old and I were about ten years old. She let dad know what mom had done. She told dad that the puppy had stinked on the floor and mommy had taken a broom handle and we watched her as she beat the dog. Dad knew his little girl was not lying. When dad confronted mom, she tried to hit Tabitha but dad wouldn't let her.

Mom and dad began fighting more and more. After this, I just knew my mother and father's marriage was ending because they were now fighting almost all of the time. I remember my mom would throw things at dad such as dishes or anything else that was handy and she was able to get her hands on. Mom wasn't always truthful with dad. She would always lie to him about anything she wanted to lie about.

When Maranda was born, my father had signed her birth certificate but by this time Maranda knew that my father was not her biological father. By the time she reached the age of sixteen or seventeen she was stealing, telling lies, and running away from home. This made my father hurt and cringe. The child he had raised as his own for the past seventeen years now hated him. Whenever dad tried to discipline Maranda, Vivian, or Bradly my mother set him straight. This was not to happen! This hurt dad even more. Maranda had gotten herself into so much trouble the state of Ohio told my mother she needed professional help. She had tried to kill herself several times. When Maranda was asked why she would lie, steal, and runaway, she said that she wanted to meet her real father.

So, the search began for James Stamo, her biological father, a man she had never layed her eyes on. Using information from my mother about James Stamo, a nationwide search began. Sometime, after being aired on the TV show unsolved mysteries, James Stamo called our house one evening. This just about killed my father. As a little girl I still remember my mother and Maranda making arrangements to go meet him. He was a married man now living in Denver, Colorado. Mother and Maranda had a airplane ticket that was paid for by the agency that was assisting Maranda. They thought that meeting her biological father would help her. This seemed to be what Maranda wanted more than anything in the world.

A few weeks later Maranda and mom left her remaining six children with dad in Columbus, Ohio and flew to Denver. She left Maranda with James Stamo and his wife Jamie and returned home a week later. We thought things were going to be fine until one night when we received a phone call from the Colorado police department. They had taken Maranda into custody because she had run away from James and Jamie's house. When asked why, Maranda would give no answer. It wasn't until the next day when Maranda arrived back at the airport in Columbus, Ohio when they discovered the reason.

When mom and the social worker met her she explained that she had been raped. And she stated that it was her father, James Stamo, who had raped her. The social worker made her go to the hospital where it was confirmed that she had been raped. Dad became very upset over the entire situation that it basically ended their marriage. Mom should have never gotten on that airplane. Although my dad tried to hold their marriage together it seemed something was always in the way. Both people have to work at keeping their marriage together.

For instant, my mom had, throughout the years, collected food stamps and welfare checks for us seven children. Basically, she was saying that my father didn't take care of us. Therefore, the state of Ohio began looking for my father. Now my father was a very hard worker. However, he was paid under the table for every job he did. No taxes were withheld and there was no trace of his income. He was pretty much an invisible person. He never had a driver license, but he was a darn good provider. He managed to take care of a household of nine with the money he earned. He made very good money working as a roofer. We always had a very big Christmas and big birthdays We had a big house and nice cars but all of that changed when my mother got into trouble.

I remember when mom told dad that the state's welfare agency knew that he lived in the house. Until then, dad never knew my mother was collecting food stamps and a welfare check. Whenever we needed food, my dad gave mom cash. When we needed clothes my daddy would again give her cash. However, as far as the state of Ohio was concerned, it was them that supported the Kendal & Ralph children. As a result, my father and mother were in big trouble.

They figured the only way to get out of trouble was for mom and dad to get a divorce. The plan they devised was to get a divorce and my mother to move to North Carolina, taking the children with her and leaving dad in Columbus, Ohio. Then, when the divorce became final they were to remarry there in North Carolina.

I also remember when I was little I had a friend from school named Tammy who lived a few doors down from us. Over the years she would prove to become longtime friends with the family. I know the year was 1989 in Columbus, Ohio. I remember the year very well because it was the year my grandpa died. I was not allowed to have my new friend visit me at our house as we had a death in the family.

Mom would take us children to school every day after dad went to work. Mom never worked. She would always go to Tammy's house where she would spend most of the day drinking coffee with her parents. Over the years my mother, as I have previously stated, always loved seeing someone else in misery. I am not sure to this day as to why she feels this way. You will just have to take my word on it that she was that type of person. Mom would listen to Lela and Bob Ling, Tammy's parents, as they revealed their biggest secrets.

I must admit that I feel Lela and Bob were the nastiest people I have ever seen in my life. Tammy and all her siblings would constantly have head lice and would always scratch their skin. Their house was always nasty. Whenever I visited them, it would always smell like sour milk.

While Lela shared her secrets with mom, she learned that Bob had an eye for younger girls. This made my mother start the evil gears to turning in her head. Mom went home and got straight to work.

Her plan was to coach my sisters into calling social services and file a report on Lela and Bob. Mom told my sisters no, she ordered them, to pretend they were friends with Tammy. Although Tammy was my best friend, she must have thought I was too little to make the call. Mom had my sisters tell social services that they had been told by Tammy, that her father had been having sex with her and that Tammy was afraid to let anyone know about it. After having made the phone call, mom visited Tammy's house the very next morning. This was normal as it was an everyday occurrence and they enjoyed it. When mom arrived for her daily visit, social services people also arrived.

They came in immediately and quickly called the cops on Bob. Of course, he was both surprised and arrested. This was my mother's work at its finest. As the next few days passed, Lela would sell things in their house in order to get the money needed to get Bob out of jail. After Bob posted bail, he was released but he was not allowed to come back to his house to see his kids, or his wife.

I remember this was just the first of my mother's dirty lies. The Ling family had it very hard from that point on. Bob, Tammy's father, had a hard time keeping a job. This was partially due to his hygiene and the fact the entire town believed him to be a child molester. Lela and Bob knew that they had to leave the state of Ohio. Everyone thought he had molested his daughter. The only way Bob was able to get the charges against him dismissed was when Tammy told social services that it was all a lie. She told them that she had said nothing to the persons who had filed the complaint with social services. However in reality, Tammy had never said a word to anyone. Instead, it was all my mothers' idea. Tammy only wanted her daddy back home. Lela and

Bob's plans were to gather up enough money to leave the state of Ohio. And, that is exactly what they did. The Ling's moved to North Carolina.

Chapter Two
Barely Getting By

By now my mother and father's marriage was coming to an end. Mom had kept in contact with the Ling's over the years since they had left Ohio. When we moved, the Ling's were able to quickly help us find a cheap house to rent in Ramseur, North Carolina. And, it was just a seven-minute drive from our house to their house. This was going to be our new life. As soon as we arrived to town, mom started making calls to social services here in North Carolina. She thrived off other people's pain.

Mom made me and my sisters come up with a fabricated story. This story to social services would say that Tammy and her new baby sister were being molested. Mom made up a story about how Tammy's father would masturbate on them. When mom realized I didn't know what masturbation meant, she forgot about using me in her dirty lie. Mom took my sisters to the local social services office in order for them to tell their story. Doing this was the only way for us to get on her good side. If someone would assist her in her evil scheme, they would be on her good side. And, she would be sure to use you again in order to help make her lies complete. As it would turn out, there would be many more calls to social services concerning the Ling's.

Dad stayed in Ohio while mom and we children made the move to Ramseur, North Carolina. We were in town about a month when mom and dad's divorce became final. A short six days later, mom met and married a man named Martin Major. She had only known him about two weeks. And, this is when and where I believe my life began to fall apart.

Martin Major had a daughter from a previous

relationship named Crystal. His mother who was an elderly woman lived with him sometimes. He and my mother married and we had to move into his filthy house.   Cindy had stayed and continued to rent the house mom had originally rented when we first moved to North Carolina. Maranda had moved to Greensboro, North Carolina with a friend of Martin Major's. Vivian and Bradly stayed with friends they had recently met. It seemed to me that everyone we knew and associated with was hooked on and doing drugs.

This left me, Keith Jr., and Tabitha to live with Martin and mom at his house. When we moved into Martin's house, which was just around the corner from Cindy's house. Just a brief walk from one house to the other. It wasn't the best place in the world in which to live. Mom had told us kids to not tell our father that she and Martin were married. I am not sure why but I believe it was so she could continue getting money from him.

At Martin's house he and mom had a nice large bedroom. However, me Tabitha and his daughter Crystal shared a single bed in a very small and filthy bedroom. Keith, Jr. slept on the sofa. Martin's mother had her own bedroom which they always kept neat and clean.

Martin's idea of being a stepdad wasn't much. He moved the refrigerator from the kitchen and put it in his and mom's bedroom. He also installed a lock on the fridge and moved his dishes into the bedroom. When it came time to cook, he allowed mom to bring food out to the kitchen and cook it on the stove but they would not cook anything for us.

Martin's mother was very old and the only thing she ate was special foods delivered to her by Meals on Wheels. Martin and mom qualified for food stamps because of me, Tabitha, Keith and Crystal They bought their foods with the food stamps and would cook such things as steaks, chicken and pork chops for themselves. They bought milk, bread and other staples for the fridge but we were never able to get any food from there.

We lived next door to a church that we attended every Sunday and Wednesday. We went there just too get food to eat. This is something we children did on a regular basis. We were able eat breakfast and lunch at our school's lunch room. However, there were many nights in which we had nothing to eat. Sometime, when finances would allow it, my sister Cindy would feed us kids. But, she was living in a rough time too. I remember we met some neighborhood people who allowed us to eat every now and again at their house. But, feeding four extra children could not and did not happen every night of the week.

It was a very difficult time in the lives of the Kendal kids. I just could not stand living at the Major house. It seemed that my brother and sisters and I cried all the time. Crystal didn't have to worry because she frequently visited her mother's house. While there she would get new clothes, food, and most times some money. What I wanted more than anything in the world was to move back to Ohio and live with my loving father. Martin and mom would eat food in front of us kids making us watch while not sharing or caring.

We would arrange to visit friends almost everyday just to get something to eat. I remember we were visiting a friend's house one day and knew they were headed off to church. Sandy and her four kids left home and headed to church. After they left I sneaked through the back door of her home and got into her refrigerator and stole a pack of frozen hotdogs. I'll never forget stealing those wieners so my sister, brother and I could eat.

At this point in my life I was in sixth grade. I never had clean clothes in which to wear and it was the same situation for my brother Keith and sister Tabitha. Both of them were in the fifth grade. Each of us had failed a few grades due to missing too many days of school so we were much older than the other kids in our class. I remember being in school one day and was called into the office. My other siblings were there when I arrived. Three ladies came in and told us we needed to be checked for head lice. I knew we had lice because we were a filthy family. The very words we were told by the school nurse was, "all of you are infested with head lice". This started a investigation concerning all the kids living in the Major household by the local department of social services.

When social services personnel came to visit our house they questioned as to why the refrigerator was in mom and Martin's bedroom. Mom told them it was in the bedroom because the kitchen was going to be painted. That was a lie and a very big one at that. After the investigation was completed mom and Martin made plans to move to Ohio. They put Martin's mother in a rest home and allowed Crystal to move in and live with her mother. Then they sold the house to the church that was located next door. Martin was an only child and the house belonged to his mother and father. His father was deceased and his mother was over ninety years old. She signed the house over to Martin and the church gladly bought the filthy little house from him.

Before I knew it, we were all in Ohio. That is, Martin Major, mom and the Kendal kids. It broke my heart to leave Cindy and my other sisters and brother behind in North Carolina. But, on the other hand, I was hoping to eventually live with dad and his girlfriend Connie. It had been a very long time since I had seen and spoken with dad. But, we did not have a clue as to where he was living. I have no idea as to what Martin and mom did with the money they received from the selling the house. It seems to have evaporated. We moved from North Carolina to Ohio into a one bedroom apartment with my aunt Danna. Martin and mom stayed in her bedroom while aunt Danna slept on the couch. We kids had to sleep on the cold tile floor.

It soon became time when we needed to enroll in school. Well, it never happened. Instead of attending school, we just laid around the apartment all day, every day. Eventually, Martin and aunt Danna began to argue over him needing to pay rent. This upset Martin and he just up and left her place without having another place for us to live. We were homeless with no car or food. Aunt Danna finally gave in and begged mom and Martin to come back which we did. We stayed a few weeks longer and Martin found a place for us to live. I believed life was getting better. It certainly couldn't get much worse, or so I thought.

Martin and mom found us a big house in Columbus, Ohio. Martin had taken a job working at a furniture plant. Aunt Danna knew some people and was able to convince them to donate a couch and some beds which helped us immensely. Finally, for the first time since mom and dad divorced, I had my own bedroom. Keith had his own room and so did Tabitha. Martin and mom were continuing to use drugs but he did work and having an income helped to make us happy.

Soon thereafter, Martin and mom became friends with a guy who managed a Seven-Eleven store located up the road just a brief walk from our house. The store provided Martin credit whenever he needed it. Whenever mom and Martin needed some additional store credit they would send me and Tabitha to the store. This was so the much older gentleman could rub our backs and ask what it was that we needed from his store. I was a fourteen year old girl. I was very naive and knew nothing about the relationships between a man and a woman. Whenever Martin and mom needed cigarettes they would send us girls to see the two older guys at Seven-Eleven. It was also how we were sometimes able to get something to eat. We got lunch meat, pop, chips and candy from there. Eventually, Martin stopped going to the store completely and only sent me and Tabitha. It was only when he needed beer that he would walk with us to the store. Sometimes, I believe because he brought us girls with him, Martin's tab at the store would show that he owed nothing. I always thought the guys at the store were nice men until one day when I was asked to go to the store alone.

It was during this visit that one of the men at the store touched my breasts and kissed me on my cheek. I ran all the way back to my home and cried. When I arrived home mom and Martin questioned me as to what I had done with the things they had sent me to buy at the store.

I told them what old man Shane had done to me. Martin called him on the phone. I thought that Martin would take up for me but instead, he laughed the entire time he was on the phone. After he finished talking and laughing, he hung up the phone. Martin asks me to return to the store but I refused. Martin got very angry at me and I was told go to my room. I gladly went upstairs but while there I overheard mom talking to him about me and what Shane wanted. Mom did nothing to stop Martin, she was all about pleasing him and, that's all mom wanted to do. Should mom have said anything to him, she would have been beaten up by Martin.

Looking back, the more I think about it, mom didn't care about us kids. Mom and Martin always had a way of using us kids in order to get whatever they wanted from other people. As time passed, I would get into trouble with mom and Martin if I didn't go to the Seven-Eleven. But I didn't care how badly my punishment was, I stayed away from that store.

Martin continued to work and save money until November of 1997. I remember the year very well because my mother got a phone call informing her that brother Bradly's baby girl was born. Shortly thereafter we moved from Columbus, Ohio to Wagram, North Carolina.

Chapter Three
Lies, Lies and more Lies

Mom had found a mobile home located close to where sister Vivian and her husband Randy lived. Vivian was the first of mom's kids to get married. For me, living at Wagram was like living in hell. Tabitha, Keith and I were basically living the way we did in Ramseur and in Columbus.

My sister Cindy and her boyfriend, Scott, lived in that same old house mom had originally rented when we first moved here in 1995. When Cindy discovered how we were being abused, she and Scott asks mom if we could live with her in Ramseur, a small community about seventy miles from Wagram. Mom agreed to allow the three of us to live with Cindy and Scott. But it was only on the condition they would buy her and Martin smokes and beer that she would allow us to live with her.

We loved living with Cindy and Scott. We once again were able to get good food, sleep in clean beds and wear clean clothes. Finally, we were able to smile every now and again. Cindy and Scott worked a steady job and got paid on a weekly basis. Whenever we needed anything they were able to buy it. Mom and Martin would always ask them to bring us Kendal children to see them on Fridays.

If she didn't bring us to see mom we would be taken away to live with Martin and mom and live in hell again. Mom knew when Cindy received her paycheck. Cindy would take mom the money needed to support her and Martin's bad habits. If Cindy didn't agree to do this we were ripped away from her and Scott. Basically, Cindy served as our mother. I was finally allowed to have a toothbrush and deodorant. It is something we didn't have at mom's house. And, her refrigerator was always full of good food at all times.

The only thing we were missing was an education. We never went to school. We had missed so much school moving back and forth from North Carolina and Ohio that between the schools we somehow became lost in the system. The school's never tried to find us. So here I am nearly sixteen years old, Keith is fourteen and Tabitha is about twelve and none of us has had any education. Tabitha and Keith had only completed the fourth grade and I had only completed the fifth grade. I was about a month into my sixth grade when I had to quit school altogether. I knew I should have been attending school but circumstances would never allow it to happen. My brother and all my sisters had dropped out of school. Not one of us graduated from school. Heck, we didn't even finish elementary school. I guess we had to be like our mother and father, for they never graduated either.

When we lived with Cindy and Scott our lives were easier. But, mom and Martin were getting to the point they demanded more money as well as other things from Cindy. They would ask for stuff like toilet paper, soap, shampoo, and just about anything else that you could imagine. Of course, this was taking money away from Cindy, Scott and us three children that we needed to live. Life with and around mom and Martin was unbearable and I knew that I had to find a way to get away from the both of them.

One evening Cindy told me that Scott had a friend who wanted to take me on a date. They knew this friend for about a year or so and his name was Chad Kevin. I had never been on a date before in my entire life and I didn't really want to go with him this time. I finally agreed to go on a dinner date with him.

During dinner I told Chad about all of my troubles. He was quick to inform me that in the state of North Carolina, I could leave home at the age of sixteen. Sure enough that just so happened to be the law. I had never felt so happy in all my life to know I could be free of my life in hell with my mother. I loved mom but she just didn't seem to love me or any of her kids. If she did, she sure had a funny way of showing it.

After having only a few dates with Chad I thought I knew the world. Here I am just sixteen years old and I wanted to be with Chad all the time. As time passed mom and Cindy got into an argument as to why I had not been with her when she came to visit each week. Mom drove to Cindy's house with the intention of taking me with her back to her house in Wagram. When I told her I was not going back with her, she smacked me around saying that I was her kid not Cindy's. It was then that I reminded her of the law. She in turn called the law on me. When the police arrived they explained to mom that the law allowed me to stay away if I wanted to and that she could no longer make me go anywhere.

This made mom upset with both me and Cindy. Mom and Martin took Tabitha and Keith, Jr. with them leaving me to witness Cindy and Scott crying because they knew full well mom and Martin would most surely abuse both of them. Cindy's landlord had seen all the cops at the house they were renting and I was asked to leave.

Well, I did just that. I left with Chad while only knowing him for one year. We moved my things into his apartment. He worked long hours with Scott as a welder in Staley, North Carolina. After only a few short months of me moving in with Chad, I became pregnant. Here I am only seventeen years old and I had no idea as to what was going to happen.

A few days passed by until I could finally break the news to Cindy that I was going to be a mother. First, I needed to find out for sure. I went to the local health department and they confirmed that I was about six weeks pregnant. I knew it was not going to be easy for me to tell the person who did care for me, who took me from the pits of hell, to help me. Later that evening, after finding out from the health department, I waited for Chad and Scott to go to work. Then, I called Cindy to our place and told her that she was going to be a auntie. Cindy wasn't too happy but she and I both agreed that we needed to tell mom I was pregnant. I let Cindy know the health department had looked up my name and said my mother was drawing food stamps for me and had a medicaid card issued in my name in Wagram seventy miles away. I explained to her that I needed the medicaid card so that I could get proper care for me and the baby.

She said that I needed to tell mom immediately. She put me in her car and we drove to mom's house late that night. Cindy told me to tell mom why we were there. I told mom and Martin that I needed my medical card for doctor visits. Of course, mom said NO! I told her it was important and that I also needed my original birth certificate and social security card. When she asked why I needed them told I her that I was pregnant.

Mom stood up beside the couch, walked over to me and proceeded to throw me against the wall with her hands around my neck choking me. Bradly, Cindy, and Tabitha struggled to pull her off of me. She finally released me and I ran out of the house and down the street where I stayed until Cindy came after me. I should have known better than to try and talk to someone who was jacked up on drugs. I never walked back into that house again. Cindy told mom that unless Tabitha and Keith could come and live with her full time, she would press assault charges on her for what she had done to me. When Cindy drove down the road to get me she had Tabitha and Keith in the car with her. This made me very happy. I had made up my mind that I was never again going to let mom control me.

During my entire pregnancy, I had a very easy time carrying the baby. In fact, I had no complications whatsoever. I discovered the baby would be a boy. During this time, in September of 1998, my brother Bradly and his girlfriend had their second child. It was a boy and they named him Bradly, Jr.

In November of 1998, Chad's grandfather bought us a brand new home. It was a mobile home but it was brand new. Grandfather John filled it with new furniture. Everything in my life was as perfect as life could be. However, a few months later in the month of January things changed for me and my family. You see, I knew my new baby would be born in January of 1999. But in December 1998, Cindy, Scott and Tabitha drove to Columbus, Ohio where they searched through out the family and located my father that we had not seen in several years.

Dad always loved drinking beer. One evening they got dad intoxicated, and put him in the car and drove him back to Ramseur, North Carolina. It was an eight-hour trip which they had driven so dad could see his first grandchild. It wasn't my idea. In fact, I never knew they had found dad until he was already in the car on the way to North Carolina. A few short weeks later, on the 11th of January, I went into labor with my son. Cory Jacob Kendal Kevin was born the next morning at 1:41 AM, January 12, 1999. It was a snowy Tuesday morning. Chad was in the room with me when Cory was born. Bradly's girlfriend, Amy Murry, stood next to me during the entire time that I was delivering Cory. Dad was one of the forty-two people to see baby Cory that morning.

The next day Cory and I were leaving the hospital heading home. I was so proud and was showing him to everyone. When we arrived home Chad and I were greeted by Cindy and my father and mother. They were sitting in their car in our driveway. Somehow, mom had discovered I was being discharged and she wanted to stay the night and see the baby since she was not at the hospital to see him. Dad said he wanted to spend time with his grandson as he had planned on leaving the following day. Martin Major, mom's current husband, had stayed at their house in Wagram as he and I did not get along very well. Mom lied to him saying she was staying in order to help me with the baby. Later that night we all went to bed. Although the baby had his own room, Cory stayed in a bassinet the first few weeks in the room with me and Chad. Mom and dad were assigned separate guest rooms. However, sometime during the night they ended up in the same room. I overheard them having intercourse throughout the night. The next morning I asked Chad to call Cindy and have her and Scott to come and get mom and dad.

Dad and mom had not seen each other since 1995 when their divorce had become final. However, that was no excuse for them to be cheating on the people waiting for them at home. On January 14th dad was put on a Greyhound bus for the trip back to Columbus, Ohio. Mom returned home to Martin as though nothing had ever happened. Finally, my life was wonderful again. I had this precious little baby boy who trusted me to take care of him.

As a few months went by I begin hearing rumors and discovered that Chad was on drugs. I found this out through Cindy's boyfriend Scott. Scott said that while he and Chad were working together he would see people come to his work and sell drugs to Chad. On a few occasions Scott said that Chad had asked him if he would sell some of his urine to him so that he could pass his drug test. With all the evidence I had gathered on Chad, I decided that I needed to confront him. So I did. While asking him about all the rumors I had heard, he confessed and said it was all true.

Not wanting to have me and my son around drugs, I left Chad and moved in with Cindy and Scott. After a few months had passed, Scott had convinced Cindy he had not seen any drug dealers meeting with Chad while at work. Joy, Chad's mother, had let me know he had been attending church on a steady basis. Therefore, I agreed that Chad and I would try living together one more time. I was determined that my baby would not have to live around drugs the way I had to do while growing up.

Cory and I moved back into the house with Chad. Cindy was in agreement with me that I should allow Chad a second chance, so I did. Things went well for about two weeks when one weekend, Cindy came to get Cory and I so we could have lunch and do some shopping together. We left the house early that morning and spent the day together. When I returned home that evening and walked through the front door I discovered our home completely bare of any furniture.

The house was totally empty. The beds, the couch, sofa, kitchen table, washing machine, clothes dryer, dressers, my baby's bed, my baby's clothing and my clothing were all gone. Chad was there but he had been badly beaten. When I asked what had happened, he stated he owed money to some drug dealers and they had come to collect. Even my baby's milk that WIC had paid for was gone. The only thing we had was the clothes on our backs and the clothes in Cory's diaper bag which had been with me that day. I waited enough time for Cindy to get home and I called her requesting that she come back and get me and Cory. This most definitely ended mine and Chad's relationship

Once I knew our relationship was over, it became much easier for me to stay away from Chad. Cory and I lived with Cindy and I began working at a Subway restaurant while making Chad pay child support.

Shortly thereafter, I discovered Chad was in jail. He had resorted to criminal acts such as breaking and entering and stealing anything he could get his hands on in order to support his drug habits. Eventually he was sentenced by the courts for the many crimes he had committed. Writing me from prison, Chad told me he wanted to see his child.

I refused. I would never take Cory to see his father. I even refused to accept phone calls from him while he was confined in jail or any other time following our break-up. This was most certainly the very end to our relationship. I knew that I could not ever have any type of relationship or live with this drug addict again.

Leaving Cory's father did not mean that it would end my relationship with his grandmother. I recall that Joy had asked me on many occasions to sign custody of Cory over to her but I refused to even consider such a thing. Although grandma Joy seemed to have a bank full of money and was very well educated, I was nothing like her or their family. I was simply a young girl on welfare and it seemed that no matter how much I worked I could not afford to support Cory and myself. I needed Chad's child support payments to help support us. But the child support payments ceased when he went to prison. To this day, eighteen years later, Cory has never laid eyes on his father. I always felt that Chad would resurface when Cory reached his eighteenth birthday. But, as of yet, that has never happened.

Mom and Martin Major's marriage was now on the rocks. Martin discovered mom had cheated on him when my father came to town for Cory's birth. Martin stayed in North Carolina while mom went for a two week visit with family in West Virginia. While there, she stayed with dad's sister.

Just because dad and mom were no longer married, did not mean aunt Marie and uncle Eugene had stopped loving the Kendal children. Mom was still welcome at their home. This is where mom stayed during her and Martin's two-week separation.

My aunt and uncle lived in a small Mingo County, West Virginia community called Dan's Branch. It is located about five miles from the city of Williamson which is the county seat. They lived, just barely getting by, on a meager social security income. My cousins worked part time digging graves for one of the local funeral homes in Williamson. Once again, mom had quickly thought of a scheme in order to get some attention. She never once considered the can of worms she was fixing to open would backfire on her at some later date.

Mom had paid my cousins, who worked at the funeral home, to somehow run a advertisement in the local news paper saying she was pregnant and that she had given birth to a baby boy and, it's father was Martin Majors. Of course, this was a whopper of a lie. Mom's tubes had been tied in March of 1984, following Tabitha's birth.

Anyhow, my cousins got the job done. This was a perfect way to win back Martin's heart. Mom knew her lies were sure to work and pull at Martins heart strings. Mom went back home to North Carolina and told Martin they needed to talk. She let Martin know that she had been admitted to the hospital while in West Virginia and she had given birth to his child. She presented Martin with the false obituary that my cousins had managed to produce while working at the funeral home. He was very sad and upset that his child had died. He believed every word of mom's story. Mom watched, uncaring, while he cried his eyes out over the death of his son. The obituary stated that Martin Major was the father and the baby's name was Lindsey Monroe Majors which is the name of Martin's father. It worked, for Martin forgot all about how mom had cheated on him. He was still in love with mom. This time more than before.

Things were fine between them until an anonymous letter arrived at Martin's house stating it was all a lie. It stated that mom had paid her nephews in West Virginia to come up with this terrible lie. There was proof mom had paid them. It was my nephews who had written the letter to Martin. They felt remorse for what they had done and admitted to Martin that mom had paid them to help make up the false obituary. This put an end to his and mom's relationship & marriage.

Chapter Four
Lilly Michelle

After I became single again due to my break up with Chad, I once again find myself living with Cindy and Scott. The four of us lived in a one bedroom apartment. They allowed Cory and I to have the bedroom while they slept on the living room sofa. A guy named Logan lived next door to us. He and Scott worked together. Later, I discovered that he had been the guy who replaced Chad when he had gotten fired from his job.

Logan was not married however he had a three year old son and his son lived with it's mother. Logan was about forty-nine years old and I am only eighteen. Cindy, Scott and I became friends with Logan.

It wasn't long before Logan and I became more than friends. He made it very clear to me that he did not want any more kids. He knew I was a single mother and did not mind helping me with Cory. The love that Logan showed for Cory made me like him even more. Cory and I moved in with Logan and he bought anything and everything that Cory and I needed. Shortly thereafter Logan received a better job offer with a construction company located in Reidsville, North Carolina. It is a small town sixty miles from where we were living in Ramseur. He took the job and Logan and I, along with baby Cory, made the move to Reidsville. We got settled in and things went very well. I no longer had to live with the frequent threats made by Chad's mother concerning her grandson.

The year 1999 is over. It is the middle of 2000 and I am nineteen. We have a nice home and my baby was now a toddler. However a few months later, in September I knew my body was changing. I went to a doctor only to find out that I was once again pregnant. Although I knew

Logan did not want any more children, I told him that I was pregnant.

When I told him that I was pregnant he seemed OK with it. We never spoke about not having the baby. I broke the news to my family. At this point in life my family members were scattered everywhere. Throughout my pregnancy, I was unable to see any of my family as the travel time and expense were too great.

During my pregnancy I received word from my family that my uncle Danny and aunt Dorothy had been arrested in Ohio for the death of their four year old daughter. Uncle Danny is mom's brother. I learned that he and Dorothy had several children in Columbus, Ohio. They had one child, a daughter, which no one had seen in over a year. The Franklin County department of social services conducted a welfare check of the children at which time they discovered Susan Jamie was missing. When they could not produce Susan Jamie, detectives in Franklin County showed up at their home to search for her.

They used a dog to track the scent of the child. The dog went straight to the basement. Once it got to the basement, it began barking at the basement wall. They brought in another dog the very same day. The second dog did the same thing. This was enough evidence to tear down the wall. They could do nothing but watch as the police moved in on the basement of his home. They broke through the concrete wall to get inside where they found a wooden box. The police department carefully removed the box, setting it on the basement floor where they opened the box and found a child's body inside.

The Hammonds were quickly placed under

arrest and taken away. The other children in their home were taken away. Danny and Dorothy Hammond were questioned by the police at which time they spilled their guts. Telling how and why their daughter was in the box they found behind the basement wall.

Danny explained that his daughter began eating paint chips from the window seal and facings. Susan Jamie's autopsy agreed with his statement. She had died of lead poisoning. Uncle Danny and aunt Dorothy were both sent to prison. I found out through conversations with family members that while in prison, Dorothy had gotten into skirmishes and her nose had been broken several times. No doubt, it is because other prisoners do not like child molesters and child murders. At home Logan and I were centering our time around the baby that was soon to be born.

Logan and I bought the things we would need like bottles, clothes, and a bed. Practically anything we thought the baby would need. I even had a baby shower where I received many great gifts for our baby. I was ready to find out the sex of the new baby inside me. I already had a son and Logan had a son from a previous relationship. All I thought about was a little girl. The day finally arrived when I would find out it's sex. I assumed that Logan would go with me that day but that didn't happen. I was all alone the day I found out that I was having a GIRL. I was a little upset with Logan because I had to go alone, but finding out our baby was going to be a girl made my day.

During the next few months as I got closer to the delivery date I became more and more excited. It is now 2001 and regardless of how much I thought about my sisters and brothers in the many different places in which they lived in North Carolina, I thought about my kids much more. When it got closer to my due date Cindy had suggested that she keep Cory until the baby was born. I made the necessary arrangements to take Cory and allow him to spend time with her about a week before the baby was born.

I began having labor pains a few times before the baby was born and would have to go to the hospital. This happened twice. Each time Logan would get very upset because the hospital sent me home after he had been sitting in the emergency room most of the day.

It was early morning of Friday, June the 8th that I had told Logan I had been awake and suffered pain throughout the night adding that I needed to go to the hospital. Logan argued with me saying he wouldn't take me because I would just get sent home again. I knew this labor pain was different than when I had Cory. After convincing him I was in labor we headed to the hospital, arriving just after 7 AM. We were informed that this would in fact be the day our baby would be born. I was indeed in labor. I slept in my room off and on until it became time to deliver my baby. She was much bigger than my first. I had a successful delivery at 11:17 AM on June 8, 2001. It was a baby girl weighing in at seven pounds and four ounces.

All the doctors left leaving Logan and I alone in the room. Logan told me he needed to go to work and he would see me the next morning. The next morning was a Saturday and Logan did not arrive until late in the afternoon. When he walked into the room I asked him if he wanted to hold his daughter. He said we needed to talk about us and the baby. When I asked what was on his mind he began and I permitted him to talk without interruption. The very next thing out of his mouth was..... **"IF YOU LEAVE THIS HOSPITAL WITH THIS BABY YOU CANNOT COME TO MY HOUSE!"** My heart dropped! I started crying while at that same moment a nurse walked in and made Logan leave the room.

I overheard him screaming at the hospital staff from wherever he was down the hallway. They ordered him to leave the hospital and not return until he could be nice. All the while, I had a few nurses come into my room and ask me what had caused me to get upset. I would not tell them why I was upset and crying.

A few hours passed by when my phone in my room rang. It was Logan. He was ready to talk nice. He said if I kept the baby, he would not pay any child support and swore to me he would stay in jail rather than provide any support for our baby. He then asked me to give her up for adoption.

I could not believe what I was hearing! Why not tell me sometime during the nine months of my pregnancy instead of waiting for her to be born? For some reason unknown to me, he could not find the time during the nine months I was pregnant to say this to me. This was not good at all! Somehow, Logan had convinced the hospital staff to allow him visit me again. The evening he visited was June 9th. He arrived at the women & children's hospital where I had been admitted. However they would only allow Logan to talk to me with a nurse present.

Logan explained to me as to how I could not afford to provide for this baby on my own. He reminded me as to how I had struggled with Cory and wished there had been some type of child support for him. Yes, this was true and every since of word, but I didn't want my daughter to go to a stranger. I told Logan the only way I would agree to adoption was if my sister would adopt her. Logan said no! No way! Logan had consulted with the adoption agency without my knowledge or permission and had requested that some of their personnel visit me at the hospital.

While Logan, the nurse and I were in my hospital room, the adoption agency personnel showed up. They let me know how the adoption process went adding that many people do it all the time.

The hospital personnel made everyone clear my room. Logan and I were not married therefore I had complete control of this baby. The nurses asks me if Logan had been threatening me in order to convince me to accept this adoption. I was so out of my mind. As night drew near, the adoption agency informed me they would be back in the morning so we could discuss it in more detail.

The hospital personnel asked me to name the baby. It was Sunday, June 10, 2001. It was my birthday! I decided to name my daughter Lilly Michelle Kendal. I couldn't think of a better name for her. Around 9:00 AM that day Logan and the adoption agency personnel came for another visit. I had already named our baby and Logan had not seen her since she was born two days ago on Friday.

Within the hour Logan had me convinced that he loved me and knew what was best for me and our baby's future. But, it would turn out to be the biggest mistake I would ever make. I signed the adoption papers. Logan looked relieved. Afterwards, I remember feeling extremely numb. Like I had made a very big mistake.

The adoption agency personnel explained to me and Logan that in the state of North Carolina the rule of adoption was, if I wanted the baby back I would have fourteen days to sign and get her back. However, if I did take her back and then return her to them again then the fourteen day rule would no longer apply. It was time for me to say goodbye to baby Lilly Michelle. I was told I could keep little Lilly in my room for about a hour until the adoption agency compiled all necessary paper work and got it notarized.

Due to it being a Sunday, it became a waiting game for the agency to get one of their people to notarize the papers. I sat alone in a wheelchair at the window in my room holding baby Lilly. Logan still refused to take even one picture of her or to even look at her. He stayed away from the hospital until the time came to pick me up. The personnel from the agency came to let me know they had found a notary.

After I signed the papers I would be separated from my daughter. Then they called Logan and he signed the papers. I still had the baby in my arms when they brought me the papers to sign. Logan is still in the hallway waiting on me to sign away our little girl. The hospital staff stayed with me during the entire time knowing full well that I did not want to do this.

I remember laying Lilly down and then I was immediately handed paper after paper in which to sign. As quickly as I would sign one, they notarized it. It only took about ten minutes to sign away my baby girl. After I was done with my last signature, I was permitted to hold Lilly one last time but only for about a minute.

A lady asked me to lay the baby down as it was time for me to be discharged from the hospital. I laid her down and sat back down in a wheelchair too numb to speak. I was then wheeled out of the room. Outside of my room the adoption agency personnel were waiting to go inside and claim the prize which they had just won.

Logan and the nurse walked me down the hall to the car. All this time I was crying, but there was nothing I could do. We finally left the hospital with Logan mumbling something from the seat next to me. I hated his guts! I could no longer stand him! I remember getting a shot to make me calm down before I left. I believe that is what made me so calm.

When we arrived home my family still had no idea that I even had my baby. I could not call anyone from my hospital room because it would have been a long distant call and the hospital phones were set up so as not to permit outgoing long distant calls.

As night time fell I cried more and more, wondering about my baby. The next morning, Monday, June 11th, I desperately hoped Logan would go to work just so I could be away from him. However, he stayed home saying he felt he needed to babysit me since I was still out of my mind following today's events concerning our baby girl. I remember not eating anything that entire day. I slept on the bedroom floor that was supposed to have been our baby's nursery. The following morning on the 12th of June, Logan got up and went to work. I felt a bit of relief knowing I didn't have to look at the man I now hated. Logan left for work and I quickly thought of a plan.

My plan was to go and get my daughter back. I didn't have a car and I have never had a driver license.

Logan never allowed me to get one. I began walking to a pay phone. I walked about two miles before finding a phone booth. I called the adoption agency and told I them wanted my child back. That is all I had to say. They gave me an appointed time and told me to bring a car seat and my picture identification and I could get her back.

While walking back home a neighbor recognized me and picked me up. She asked as to when my baby had been born. I poured my whole heart out to her as she drove me home. She said she would have her husband pick me up later and take me to the adoption agency. She further agreed he could drive me the seventy miles to my sisters house. So, that started my plan into action. It was around noon that day and I knew monster Logan would not be home until around 5 O'clock PM.

I went home and wrote Logan a letter to inform him that I'm going to get my daughter, not his. I hated him so much for the way he did me. I packed my bags and what baby clothes I did have and then waited on my neighbor's husband to come pick me up.

We arrived at the adoption agency about a hour later. I walked in and they brought my Lilly to me from somewhere in a back room. I felt whole again. I felt as though this whole adoption thing had never happened. Lilly Michelle was wearing a mint green dress with pink roses and little pink socks. She definitely did not look like the same baby that I had given birth to a few days earlier. She was not red in her face like she was when she was born. The adoption agency handed me some diapers and wipes for the baby in hopes it would help me.

I left very quickly with my daughter and I knew that I would never mention Lilly's adoption to anyone. I had her back and that was all that mattered. My neighbor drove us to Cindy's house in Ramseur. Cindy was the first in my family to see my newborn baby. We spent the evening showing off my baby to the entire family. Everyone adored Little Lilly.

The phone rang at Cindy's house. It was monster Logan calling to tell Cindy all about the baby's adoption and my letter he had found. I felt so betrayed! The rumor spread like a wildfire throughout my family and suddenly, they just didn't want me around anymore.

During the next few days I was severely judged by my family concerning the adoption. Scott and Cindy said I could no longer stay with them. I let them know that I would be gone the next day. The next morning while everyone was asleep, I took my children and left. I had made arrangements with Cindy's landlord to take me to a woman's shelter. And, as I rode in the van from Ramseur to Greensboro, I began to realize that maybe adoption was the best thing for baby Lilly Michelle.

I made a quick decision to stop by the adoption agency and once again turn my baby girl over to the state of North Carolina. The agency personnel and I spoke for about a hour, convincing me that my baby would have everything she would ever dream of having. She would not want for anything during her entire life. They also told me that state regulations for North Carolina allowed for her to be given a new name since she was under three months old. And that she would be given a new birth certificate. The agency kept all the hospital bands that was on her arm when she was born to give to her new family. It was a very sad time for me but I was convinced she would have a better life than I could provide for her.

So, I signed away my rights once again. I was told that I could never get her back again. I took a camera with me and made sure that I took some pictures of her with her brother Cory. Of course, Cory did not understand anything that had happened. I quickly walked away and left the agency. It was the last time that I saw my daughter Lilly Michelle. It was hard to hold back the many tears but I had to think of Cory as well as myself.

When we left the adoption agency and went directly to the woman's shelter in Greensboro, North Carolina. It is located about a twenty minute drive from the adoption agency. When my sister's landlord dropped me and Cory off he let me know that he would not let anyone in my family know where we were.

My family was so corrupt, it wasn't even funny. They always managed to do terrible things to each other just to watch them hurt. They would do things such as calling the cops on each other or calling social services on each other and filing a false complaints just because they wanted to watch someone suffer. Instead of helping someone they would much rather hurt them. It seems that feeding on other people's pain was the only way they could survive. This has made me develop a sad and negative feeling toward most everyone in my family. It has caused me to not want to be around any of them.

This meant that Cory and I were on our own. His father was still in prison. Dad was living somewhere in Ohio and never knew I had a daughter. Mom had filed for divorce from Martin Majors and was living with another man named Luke Wayne. Cindy and Scott had moved to Washington state in Pierce County where Scott's brother and sister-in-law lived. Tabitha was living with mom and Luke. And, Keith Jr. was living with Rocky Love and his wife, Mary. Rocky was my sister's landlord and the person who had driven me to the adoption agency. I believe Cindy had gotten upset that Rocky had taken me to the adoption agency and as a result she and Scott made the move to the state of Washington. Bradly was living with a woman who is the mother of two of his children. Vivian was married and pregnant with her first child. Maranda was living somewhere in Greensboro, North Carolina.

Although I tried to find her while I was living in the shelter, my efforts were unsuccessful. I knew that she had two children which I had never seen. She was smarter than me as she had taken her life and left this corrupt family behind.

I was successful at getting a job while living in the shelter while Cory attended a local day care. I saved all the money I could with hopes of getting a place for me and Cory to live. Cory was potty trained so I no longer had to buy diapers. Potty training Cory was something Cindy had done for me when they had kept him the week prior to me having had baby Lilly. The only money I had to spend from my checks was the fee to cash the checks.

The day finally came that I had enough money to rent a place of my own. I knew that I had no intentions to ever live in Greensboro, North Carolina again. I tried to find sister Maranda. I knew she lived in Greensboro with her two children but I was unsuccessful at finding her.

Therefore, I packed mine and Cory's belongings and once again called on people I knew in Ramseur to come get Cory and me. I had been able to find a small mobile home at Bennett, North Carolina. One having two bedrooms. Bennett is located about fifteen miles from Ramseur. I had managed to save enough money to pay a few months rent in advance on a new place in which to live. And for once in my life I felt totally free of all the drama concerning my corrupt family.

I still did not have a driver license and I was still without an education. These were two big disadvantages when seeking employment. Rumor spread like wildfire in our little town that I was back in town. Mom and Luke Wayne along with Tabitha also began looking for a place to live. It just so happens they landed a nice place next door to me and Cory. The same landlord owned both places. Luke Wayne started a new job at Brady Lumber which is located about ten minutes away. He depended upon a friend to drive him to and from work as Luke did not have a driver license. By living next door to mom I would visit them often. They were small visits as I could only tolerate mom for a very short period of time. It wasn't that I hated mom but I knew how she was. She got her way all the time or the persons who were around her paid dearly. She seemed always to be a very vindictive person.

As fall 2001 creped by, I stayed at the mobile home although I knew that I needed to find a job and a ride to and from work for me and a ride to daycare for Cody as he had not yet attained school age. All my siblings had a driver license. I was now twenty years old with only a fifth grade education and still no driver license. I could barely read and write. I also have problems with my math skills. The words that I did know were learned while I was at the woman's shelter where they taught me what little reading skills I now have. Due to my educational level, it was impossible for me to pass a test to get my driver license. I just could not read. I blame my mother for my lack of schooling. She could have allowed me; no she should have made me, to go to school but she didn't. I was hurting once again. I was going to lose the place that I had struggled so hard to get. I knew something had to change.

Chapter Five
Meeting The Devil

At the end of 2001 I eventually lost the place that I had rented for failure to make my rent payments. I was forced to move in with mom next door. I felt there just had to be another way out for me. As things would turn out, the guy that Luke was working with and providing for Luke's transportation to and from work everyday, thought it would be a great idea to take me out on a date.

Brad Joe Samuel knew how much I disliked living with my family and their way of life. After going out with him every night after work he asked me to move into his place. Since he was living in a one bedroom apartment I turned him down even though I so badly wanted to leave mom's place. I explained to Brad that I couldn't live with him and my son Cory in a one bedroom place. Brad asked me if he would get a larger place in which to live would we move in with him. I said yes, while really not thinking about it too much. Two days later he asks if Cory and I would to go for a car ride with him.

I agreed and we drove about fifteen miles up the road where he pulled into the driveway of a very nice mobile home. He handed me a set of keys saying that it was our place. He told me how much he knew I had wanted to leave mom and Luke's place and further stated that he loved me very much. Of course, I accepted his offer and moved in with him. I was very much relieved to know the two short weeks I was forced to live with my mother was over.

Once I accepted Brad's offer and moved in with him, a whole new life began for us. While living with Brad, I soon became pregnant for the third time. Brad was so very happy. In fact, happy wasn't the word for it. I just hoped everything would work out for us in this new relationship. As the year of 2002 arrived, we soon discovered we were having a boy. It was from the very beginning that we decided Brad Joe, Jr. was to be his name. Brad and I both wanted it very much. Finally, we agreed on something. Things were great in the beginning but I soon discovered that Brad had a drinking problem. Like my dad, he loved drinking beer. I was not then nor was I ever a drinker or smoker. And, it was because of this, that I didn't quite fit in with Brad and the people who where his family and friends.

Brad and, I like anyone else, would have discussions and disagreements concerning events in our household. Although he would become very angry at times, we would never become physical with each other. Whenever our disagreements became too large, I would simply leave. Either I would have one of my sisters to come get me and Cory, or Brad would take us to one of them. During such times, I would stay gone for weeks at a time thinking that I would teach him a lesson to not get angry and yell at me whenever he drank.

When getting closer to my delivery due date, I heard rumors that Brad had told half of the people in our small town that he was going to take his son away from me after it was born. I knew this could not be a possibility because he was a very severe alcoholic. Often times he would wake up and begin drinking before leaving for work. Each time I would leave, Brad would beg for me to return and I would eventually go back to him. I guess it is because I have always had a very forgiving heart and I definitely did not like living with family members.

I was not the only one of mom's children having babies. It seems she was having grandbabies right and left. All my sisters and brothers were becoming parents. By July sister Cindy had her first child. He was a small baby, born prematurely, and weighing in at a little more than three pounds and eight ounces. I know this because I was there when he was born. The very next day on July 3rd, Bradly's wife, Amy, had a baby girl. Then on Friday, August 16th, 2002, at 3:58 PM, my Brad Joe, Jr. came into this world. He was a healthy baby weighing in at six pounds and nine ounces.

I was yet again in love. I couldn't say officially that I had three babies, as I only had two with me. Brad and I argued many, many times as his parents wanted Brad, Jr. to live with them. I could not agree to this as his entire family drank much like he did. It soon became clear to me that he and I could never get along so, once again, I left. This time Cindy had no room for me and my family because she was now a mother of a unhealthy baby who was still in the hospital.

Once again, I was forced to move in with mom and her boyfriend, Luke Wayne. I was dead set against it but felt I had no other choice. Cory, Brad Jr and I stayed at mom's place until someone called the department of social services and filed a false complaint against me and our living conditions. I later discovered that it had been someone in Brad's family who had filed the false complaint. Social services personnel conducted a home visit at mom's place after which they realized that I had everything I needed for the kids and they immediately closed the case.

While we were staying at mom's place, Brad would see Luke while they were at work and he would tell Luke that he wanted to see the kids. I permitted him to come by mom's place and visit the kids while they were playing outside in the yard. He seemed sincere about wanting to stop drinking, going to church and, helping me in my efforts to get a driver license. He said he would do all this if I would just come back home. I believed him and decided to move back in with him.

I had Cindy to drive me and the boys back home however, for some reason unknown to me, Brad was not home when we arrived. Cindy could not stay with us as she had to get back to her child that had finally been released from the hospital. I waited on the porch with my boys until Brad arrived. We sat outside waiting on him for more than three hours.

Once Brad arrived, we all went inside the trailer where I sat Brad, Jr, while still in his car seat, on the living room floor and went directly to the bathroom. It seems I had not used the bathroom in hours. Immediately thereafter, Cory ran to me and told me that Brad had just taken the baby out of the house and left. I ran outside but Brad had already gone with our son. He had tricked me into coming home so he could take our baby.

He took our son to his sister's house and left him with her. She had several daughters as well as their drug dealing boyfriends living with her. I was extremely upset to have again been betrayed by a man who I thought had loved me. I called the police and they came to the trailer. However, it just so happens the police officer who came was Brad's cousin.

Soon, Brad pulled into the driveway without my son. I was determined that I was going to kill him for what he had done. I felt so angry and betrayed. Brad talked with his cousin, the police officer, telling him that he paid all the bills for the household and that he wanted me gone. The officer asked me if I paid any of the bills and I said no. I further stated that I had just delivered a new baby a few months ago and I did not work. The policemen then asked me to leave. I told them that I would leave but only after Brad gave my son back to me.

Brad lied to the police officers telling them that it had been days without me having been with our baby. He further stated that I had abandoned him. Once again, the officers asks me to leave. I let them know that I was not going to leave without my son. They ordered me to walk outside and leave. I looked Brad in the eyes and told him that if I ever got my hands on him I would kill him and, I meant every word of it.

Brad's cousin immediately put handcuffs on me and proceeded to read me my rights. I should never have threatened to kill him especially with witnesses present. They put me in a police cruiser along with my son Cory sitting on my lap. We sat in the cruiser until my sister Vivian and her husband Randy arrived to get Cory. I was then transported to the Moore County jail located in Carthage, North Carolina.

It was the first time that I had ever been arrested and I had no idea what to expect. It was on a Friday evening when I arrived and was booked at the jail. The jail staff took my picture and finger prints. I had blood drawn in jail in order to test me for diseases and other such things. Later that night a lady in the nurse's area told me that my blood test came back fine and no diseases were detected. Of course, I already knew that. However, she did tell me something that I did not know. She told me that I was pregnant! I just absolutely could not believe it. Since it was Friday, I had to spend the weekend as well as Monday in jail.

On Tuesday morning, the ladies in jail who had been telling me what to expect when it was my turn to see a judge, told me that I should expect to be released. Soon, my name was called at which time I had to line up with four other women. The five of us were chained to each other after which we walked from the jail to the court house. I spoke to the judge as did the other four women.

The judge told me to stay away from Mr. Brad Joe Samuel. He further stated that if I went back around him I would be arrested again. The judge also let Brad know that I was pregnant and would be having another baby. This time Brad did not have the same smile on his face as when we found out we were pregnant with Brad, Jr.

The judge asked me as to why I felt a need or desire to kill Brad and I stated that it was because he took my son away and that he had lied to me. The judge instructed me to obtain a custody lawyer. The judge then ask me if I still wanted to kill Brad Samuel. I looked straight at him and said absolutely! The judge told me that he admired my honesty but that I could not say things like that. Just when I thought things could not get worse, Brad's mom and dad were in the courtroom. And, they had their attorney present. They had petitioned the court for sole custody of Brad, Jr. I was ordered to stay away from them. I was escorted from the courtroom and was returned to the jail after which I got back into my street clothes and was released.

Once released, I began walking up the highway as I had no means of transportation except for my thumb and I was at least forty miles from where my family lived.

Once again, I was betrayed and screwed by someone whom I thought had loved me. To beat it all, I was now pregnant with his child and baby number four. I needed to somehow find my way back to mom's house as that is where Cory had been taken the day I was arrested. While walking down the highway, after being released, a total stranger picked me up and drove me all the way to Ramseur.

Mom and Luke had moved from Bennett back to Ramseur. Several days had passed when I was called over to my sister's house where an officer had a summons waiting for me. It was for a custody hearing concerning Brad, Jr. His grandparents, Cait and Carl were seeking full custody of him. Here they are both pushing eighty years old and they wanted full custody of my son. On the day I was to appear in court, I had no money for a lawyer. I was forced to attend the hearing or otherwise, I would have again been arrested.

When it came time to hear our case, Brad's mother and father talked about me like I was a dog. They had two attorneys which they had known for years there to represent them. The court permitted Brad to sign over his rights to his mother and father. I was determined to not give up any of my rights. I wasn't signing shit! As a result, they set a new court date which was scheduled for three weeks away. I needed a lawyer and was granted one appointed by the court. Three weeks later when court was back in session my lawyer knew that I didn't have a job, a driver license, or a home in which to live. My only income to provide for me and Cory was state welfare all the while we were living with someone else. With all this in mind, I lost custody of Brad, Jr.

Here I am pregnant with Brad's second child. I knew this man too well and I would never agree on anything with him ever again. And, I am once again living with mom and her boyfriend Luke. I had no choice but to cater to their every whim. While I was working, mom would never allow me to save any money that I would need to somehow better myself. Instead, I was required to give her money so she could buy things that she wanted. I received food stamps but it was impossible for me to buy food just for Cory and myself. Mine and Cory's food stamps were spent on steaks, soda, snacks and other groceries that mom wanted. If I refused, I knew that Cory and I would be homeless.

Brad said that I could come home to him if I wanted to. But, I didn't want to live with him again. I hated his guts, like I had learned to hate everyone else that had done me wrong. I always cried and would worry about what the next day would bring for Cory and me as well as the baby inside my belly. About a week before Brad, Jr.'s first birthday, Brad planned the party for him and it would be held at the mobile home that we had once shared. I had not seen Brad, Jr. for about nine months. Brad said if I would decorate for the party then I could come see him. Of course I immediately said yes because I missed my son so very much. Brad said if I wanted I could stay in the spare bedroom the night before his party. He also allowed my sister, Maranda, to stay so that members of his family would not be able to give me a hard time. I was a very small woman during those years and I knew Maranda would not permit anyone to bother me.

With all this in mind, we went to the trailer and

I decorated it with balloons and streamers. It did not matter that I was nine months pregnant. I was like a kid in a candy store waiting to see my son Brad, Jr. Finally, it was time for the party and company began to arrive. My son also arrived. At first, they wouldn't let me hold him but they eventually gave in and let me hold him. We sang happy birthday for him and cut his cake.

During the party I noticed Brad, Sr. was very much intoxicated. You might say that he was as drunk as a skunk! There were about sixty guests in attendance, some were inside and some were outside and all for little Brad's first birthday. Little Brad made a big mess while eating his cake. The Samuels agreed to allow me to give him a bath and clean him up. I could not believe I was finally holding the baby that I had last held nine months ago. While I was bathing little Brad, I went into active labor.

Maranda and I drove to the hospital with Brad, Sr. following close behind. Remember, he is so drunk that he could barely walk. Soon, we arrived without incident, at the hospital in Moore county. I was wheeled into the emergency room and fourteen minutes later, on little Brad's first birthday, Wade Alan Samuel entered the world at 8:12 PM on Saturday, August 16, 2003. He weighed in at six pounds and seven ounces. He had to be delivered in the emergency room as I did not have enough time to make it to the labor and delivery room.

Brad, Sr. was kicked out of the hospital until he sobered up. When I left the hospital the following Monday morning, I did not go home with Brad, Sr. That was not going to happen to me again. Instead, I went back to mom's house. This started a war between me and the

Samuel family. As it became more and more evident that I would not be returning to the Samuel's home with our new baby. They would often threaten me and sometimes they would try and follow me so they could eventually get a chance to take the baby.

Brad's family began calling social services again, saying unimaginable things about me. It is something the Samuel's family would do on a daily basis. As a result, the workers for the department of social services began multiple investigations. This time, they knew they couldn't close the case because phone calls continued to pour into their office concerning me and my boys.

Eventually, in an effort to avoid them, we left from mom's house and moved in with Tabitha. The year had ended; Halloween, Thanksgiving, Christmas and New Years Day for 2004 had passed. We were beyond my birthday in the middle of the year of 2004 and multiple calls were still being made to social services concerning me on an almost daily basis. Sometime they would total more than seven calls per day. The unimaginable things a person can falsely accuse someone of is unreal. It is terrible the things that some people can think up just to try and make a person's life, my life, a living hell. I just could not believe it. After living with Tabitha for brief period, she met a man and once again, we had to move back in with mom and Luke.

Soon 2004 past and Brad, Sr. was not allowed to visit with his son Wade. Chad was still in prison and I now have a job working at the Dollar General store located in Ramseur. While still dealing with social services, I was barely getting by on my small biweekly paychecks and welfare.

The calls to social services began to get worse. A few of their workers at a time would come to check on the health and safety of Cory and Wade. Up to now, they had not involved mom and Luke Wayne in any of the cases.   But now, social services wanted to conduct background checks on both mom and Luke. They also wanted to do one on me as well. They already knew I had been arrested a few years earlier but insisted that it would not be held against me provided everything else in my background check came back clear. I knew I had not been in any other type of trouble and that it was my only legal problem. As far as I knew, mom had never been arrested, and I believed the same concerning Luke Wayne. We all gave our consent for the background check and the workers told us they would be back the following day.

Early the next morning, the social services personnel pulled into mom and Luke's driveway. They informed me that I had new charges filed against me. I cried and ask them what I had done. They replied that I had endangered my children.

This is when I first learned that Luke Wayne had failed his background check. In conducting his background check it revealed that he was a registered sex offender and that he had been in prison for molesting his own daughter years ago. He had been also arrested, convicted and served time in prison for writing bad checks. I was astonished and just could not believe he and my mother had failed to tell me these things about him. They knew this big dark secret and could have prevented this from happening.

Now, through no fault of my own, I have been charged with endangering the health and safety my two boys along with a few other things that went along with me allowing them to be living in the dwelling with a registered sex offender. I was ordered to leave the residence of my mother and Luke Wayne.

Having no other place to go, I was forced to crawl back to Brad Samuels, Sr. Oh how I hated myself but, it was a place to live. Three days later, Brad and I had a court date. That very morning I was surprised to learn the department of social services was seeking custody of my children. As I sat next to Brad in the courtroom I was praying the judge would allow me to keep my boys. When our names were called, I crept ever so slowly to the seat where I was instructed to sit.

The judge began with Brad and ended with me. The judge listened closely to the social service employees as they submitted their case. I listened patiently while they made me out to be a piece of white trash. The judge looked at Brad and said he was a very bad alcoholic. He further stated he had proof that Brad had recently been hospitalized as the result of a drug over dose with Zanex. As a result, there was no way he was going to get custody of the kids. He asked Brad if there was anything he wanted to say and Brad answered, "No sir". The judge then ordered him to set down and shut up.

He then asks me to stand. I stood in front of a room full of people who wanted to take my kids away from me. I listened intently to the judge as he tells how I had allowed my kids to eat, sleep, live, and play in a house where a man who is a registered sex offender lived. And, how my actions had endangered them. When I tried to speak, the judge interrupted me and told me if I spoke again without his permission, I would be arrested.

With that being said, he asks me if I wanted to say anything. I answered him with an affirmative, yes. After him rolling his eyes at me, he asks what could be so important that I had the nerve enough to speak to a man who was himself a father. Further explaining how he would have never put his kids in harm's way the way that I had done. With his permission to speak, I told the judge that I did not know Luke Wayne was a sex offender. I explained that as a result, I should not be held accountable. Another complaint that I was being charged with had to do with my bringing the kids back and forth between Brad's house, Tabitha's and mom's house. Moving back and forth was evidence of my failure to provide my kids with a steady and stable home. I knew the judge had made up his mind to take my kids. Oh, it just about killed me. I ask him why and he looked at me and said Ms. Kendal when you can answer that question you can have your kids back.

He ordered that I turn over both Cory and Wayde to social services at 4:00 O'clock PM. He told me if I failed to comply with his order or if I tried to run with them I would be in a lot of trouble. Suddenly, I fainted while standing there. When I woke up I discovered they had evacuated the court house floor. I was surrounded by EMT's with my social workers close by my side. I saw Brad off a good distance from me. I was going to be transported to the hospital. The social workers told me right then and there they wanted to get the kids now and not wait until 4:00 PM as was stated in court room.

Social services personnel drove to Brad's mother and father's home to get the kids while I was on my way to the hospital. Certainly, it must have made Brad's family the happiest people on earth. They had succeeded in what they had set out to do. When I got to the hospital I thought I was having a heart attack. The EMT started an IV on me and gave me something to help me relax.

If there was any good news for me, it was that I was not having a heart attack. Instead, I had suffered a severe panic attack. I thought, how could both my boys be gone? The doctor suggested that I stay the night in the hospital as I had been given medication to keep calm.

I left the hospital the next day. Brad took me home to his place. I did not have the strength to walk and could hardly talk. I was like a zombie. The medication served to calm me down and keep me from thinking about the kids. I had no idea where they were, how they were, or when I would be able to see them again.

After a few days, I stopped taking the medication the hospital had prescribed in order to keep me calm. When I finally came to my senses, I was filthy. I had not taken a shower or bathed for a few days. Neither had I ate anything during these few days. I was hurting inside and Brad was making advances with me trying to become intimate. And, I didn't want any part of that. While fighting about it, he let me know he had been having intercourse with me during the past few days while I was drugged and unconscious. He further stated that I seemed to enjoy it. Technically, he had raped me.

If you remember, the time when Brad had taken my son Brad, Jr away from me that I had wanted to kill him. Well, my desire to kill him at this time was much greater. The following morning after Brad had left for work the social services personnel arrived unexpectedly and wanted to bargain with me.

They said that if I would leave Brad, get a place my own, and stay away from my entire family I would get my kids back. I knew that it would take time for me to prove that I would never go back to Brad or my family again. They let me know that they would help me get started. To do this, they would arrange a place for me to live at the woman's shelter until I could afford a place of my own.

I took them up on their offer and we made necessary arrangements for them to pick me up me the next morning. They explained the only thing I could take would be one suitcase. Anything my boys owned must stay. It was the month of November of 2005. During that day, after they left, I wrote a mean, ugly, note to Brad. I let him know how much he was at the top of my list of people that I hate. I had so much anger that had built up inside me for people who had betrayed me. I packed a suitcase and hid it beneath the bed hoping Brad could not find it. The following morning the social worker arrived to get me. We left about twenty minutes after Brad left for work. We then drove to a parking lot where we met a lady from the woman's shelter. The social services worker did not know where the woman's shelter was located. The lady who ran the shelter picked me up in the parking lot and we went to the shelter where she did the necessary paperwork to admit me to the shelter.

We took a tour of the house and I was made aware of all their rules. That evening I was given a note by the manager of the house saying I had to call my social services case worker before 5 PM. I called from the only phone in the place. It was a big relief to learn I was going to see my kids. It would be my first visit in over two weeks. The judge had agreed that Brad would have to make arrangements for his visits with the kids through the department of social services. This was because he had a problem with drug use as well as him being an alcoholic.

As for me, I only had make arrangements with the foster parents and could visit them as often as I wanted provided the foster parents approved the visits. This was music to my ears. I was so happy. While still thinking that I didn't deserve to have my kids taken away, my first few visits with the kids went well. I had hoped for more but I had got a job that the woman's shelter had helped me to get at a local Pizza Hut. It was a restaurant where most of the ladies living at the shelter worked.

November was ending with the Thanksgiving holiday near when the foster parents asks me if I would want to join my kids for the holiday. To make a visit and eat Thanksgiving dinner with the kids, of course I accepted the invitation without any hesitation. I had purchased a few new outfits and toys for both Cory and Wade. I felt a bit guilty spending the money I was saving but, it was spent on them. The state was making both me and Brad pay child support. He only had to pay for Wade while I was required to pay support for both Wade and Cory.

December 2005 was coming to a end and Christmas drew near. I was maintaining regular visits with the kids. Social services was allowing the kids to come and visit me at the shelter three times a week at which time they were allowed to stay with me for a few hours. The foster mother and I became close friends. Due to our friendship, I was allowed more visits than just the three times a week.

And, if I went to her house and cleaned it, I would get to see the kids even more. I was allowed to spend countless hours with the kids provided I did her laundry, folded her clothes, moping and sweeping her floors and, cleaning her toilets. It was difficult but seeing my kids made it all worthwhile. I did all this work while maintaining my regular job working at the Pizza Hut.

I was given a curfew when I moved into the shelter. I had to be home by 8:00 PM and was allowed to leave as early as 7:00 AM. I used my free time to see my boys. One morning I woke up feeling sick as a dog. I was throwing up my guts. I thought I had caught a stomach bug or the flu. I left that morning and called off work to see a doctor. Oh my gosh, I found that I was pregnant with my baby number five.

How could this be I ask myself? I had not been with any man. But soon I remembered. Back in November, when I returned from the hospital after my kids had been taken away, I was given drugs to calm me down. These drugs made me become a zombie. I now remember Brad telling me that he had intercourse with me while I was passed out due to the drugs. He had raped me as he did it while I was unconscious! I was shocked and I needed to tell my social worker because the court had ordered me to stay away from Brad.

What could I do? I made a phone call to the social worker handling my case. I had to make a visit to her office because I could not say what I wanted to say over the phone. I was given a appointment the next morning and went to the office to talk about my new problem. Once I got there, the worker and I spoke at great length. We discussed about how I needed to stay away from

Brad and that she would tell him about the pregnancy. The only way I was to see Brad, Sr was in court.

We continued going to court for now. The first time I attended court since I became pregnant with this baby, Brad handed me a letter. We were not allowed to talk. I managed to get through the day in court and the judge was much more pleasant with me as he had seen that I was very serious at trying to regain custody of my kids. He ordered me to continue to stay away from Brad and I was fine with that. Brad and I were given a long list of things to do in order to regain custody of our kids. He was required to attend rehab due to his drug use. He was also ordered to attend alcoholic anonymous. He failed to attend any of the meetings.

On the other hand, I was ordered to complete a long list of things. I had to attend and comply with any and all recommendations the state asked me to do. I was ordered to attend parenting classes. These classes consisted of a twelve week program, and I finished the program. By this time I had saved enough money to get a place for the kids and me to live. In January of 2006 I was once again able to move from the shelter into a place of my own. Social services required me to get a three bedroom place. A room for each of the kids and one for myself. In February 2006 I was told by the court that I could have the kids back. However, my case would stay active for about twelve months.

I brought the kids home to live in our new home. This was a new beginning for all of us. Finally, we were doing great. As the first month went by, I enrolled Cory in school and Wade was enrolled in preschool. I continued working. I was again working at a Dollar General store.

Being pregnant with baby number five I worked hard and was barely able to get by. In May of 2006 I received my electric bill in the mail. I knew something was terribly wrong as when I opened it. I found it to be over eleven hundred dollars! I knew this could not be correct. I called the power company and they told me they would cut off my power if I couldn't pay my bill. I then talked with another power company employee about my bill and ask why it was so high. I was told that it was because I had four mobile homes on my power bill. They further explained that three of the mobile home accounts were for homes located in the trailer court where Brad lived. They told me I had given them permission to use my social security card and birth date to connect the electric power in my name. The home that I lived in made four accounts that were in my name.

I cried so hard. I thought, was it meant for me to have a streak of bad luck to happen to me for the rest of my life? Life surely had to give me some slack somehow or sometime. It just had to. They gave me only seven days to come up with the entire past due amount of my bill. Otherwise, I would have my electricity disconnected. I had to tell my social worker and the day finally arrived I needed my power bill payment. I lost power that afternoon and before dark my kids were once again removed from the home I had worked so hard to provide for them. Oh, how I wish I had a gun! I wanted Brad Sr. dead!

My kids and I cried and cried as they were once again snatched away from me. My workers told me they were sorry adding that I needed to leave Moore County. Otherwise, when the baby I was carrying was born they would be required take him as well.

Therefore, I left Moore County and moved in with Tabitha. This move put me about two hours from the foster home where Cory and Wade were living. It's June, and we are back in court. We discussed as to why the kids are going back into foster care. I believe the judge actually felt sorry for me. He knew I had already complied with everything they had asked me to do during my previous court dates. This time I was ordered to get a driver license. I was permitted to talk with the judge and tell how I could barely read and write. I could neither read nor comprehend well enough to pass a written test. I devoted all my time at getting my kids back. I never would have believed the court would order me to get a driver license. To make it worse, I was ordered to return with it within five days. They explained that if I have a license then I would not have to depend on anyone but myself to get me to and from places. The judge stated that any other parent would have given up on their effort to regain custody of their kids. That's what made me think he truly did feel sorry for me.

I left the court house again thinking I can't do this. I was told to come back on day six and the first thing I should do is be able to show my driver license. I returned to Tabitha's house telling my entire family that I needed a license. I studied the driving manual all night long until I fell asleep from exhaustion. I awoke the next day to get ready for my driver license test. As luck would have it, I was read the questions by the license agency employee. I had help reading, but I was required to do the answers on my own. I passed the test and left that day, the fifth of June in 2006, with my driver license. I went to court and showed them I had my license.

If it wasn't one thing it was another. Whenever I completed something they had ask me to do, I had twenty more things to do. During my court date. They ask me to go into a special room with just my lawyer and judge. I asked the judge why couldn't my kids come live with me at Tabitha's house? I asked why my kids could not stay with my family? That is when I had finally been given an answer. I was told that both my family and Samuel family were guilty of calling social services on me. I thought, this had to be a mistake. My family wanted my kids back with me as much as I did or, so I thought. This meant war between me and my family. I went back to Tabitha's house and I was determined I would not reveal one thing about my court room findings.

It is now August, and I am now nine months pregnant. I knew I had to do something in order to get my kids back. During my last week of pregnancy, I met a man named John. He and Tabitha had known each other as friends. John and I dated each other though he knew I was pregnant. He knew about my past and promised to help me all he could. I knew very little about John. Occasionally he would give me some financial assistance which helped me to get things that I needed while I was living with Tabitha.

On Tuesday, August 8, 2006, I gave birth to a baby boy. He was my fifth child and I named him Winston Watts Samuel. He came into he world weighing six pounds and nine ounces and he was twenty inches long. And, I was told then, that he was a very healthy baby. As luck would have it, this would be prove at a future date to be not true. Winston was born at three PM and early the following morning I went to the operating room to get my tubes tied. When I woke up I remember hearing the nurse say a man named Brad Samuels came to see a child that I was claiming to be his. He wanted to hold him. But, since I was unable to give my consent, they would not allow him to hold Winston. She added that he was highly intoxicated. He got to see Winston through the glass viewing window of the hospital nursery.

As the day went on with me enjoying my new baby in my hospital room, I had a visitor. It was social services personnel who represented the county in which I had delivered the baby. They removed my son and made a phone call to Moore County. Social services personnel of Moore County told them I was safe with the baby because I had not been in court concerning the new baby like my other kids. Therefore, there was no case to open. As I left the hospital with Winston, I could not for the life of me figure out how Brad Samuels was able to find out I was giving birth to Winston. Neither did I know who had called social services on me? Who told Brad my room number? I had it fixed when I arrived at the hospital so that no one was to know my room number. No one should have known. Then, I got to thinking as to what the judge and I spoke about in that private room. How my family, in addition to Brad's family would call social services on me. That is why my boys went to foster care and not to my family. I started to realize I was telling my secrets to my family and they were using them against me. You see, my mother and Luke Wayne knew I was getting food stamps. I was constantly asked if I would buy them groceries with my food stamps? Whenever I would kindly say I am sorry I cannot do that, there would suddenly be a new phone call made to social services concerning me. When I had my tubes tied I was given pain medication. Whenever I refused to give them my pain pills, I would have more visits from social services concerning me and Winston.

Now, I have three children in two different counties in which social services were keeping a eye on. Wade & Cory are still in foster care while Winston and I were living with Tabitha. John and I began making plans to leave Tabitha's house. Tabitha was having a sexual affair with Brad Samuels boss. This is how I believe Tabitha got word to Brad that I was having his son the morning he came to the hospital.

My plan at this time was to move as far away as I could possibly get from my family. John told me that he had a place in Shallotte, North Carolina which is about four hours from where I am currently living. When Winston was just a few months old, John and I took Winston with us and moved to Shallotte.

Shallotte is a beach area. I was so happy to get away from my family. I promised myself that if this relationship did not work out I would still not return to my family. I loved my family but they did not love me. We moved to the Shallotte area on March 7, 2007. I got a job working at a movie gallery in Shallotte and began getting a weekly paycheck.

Although Wade and Cory were still in foster care, I finally had a home in which they could live. The winter months ended and spring and summer came and went. Fall was finally here. We made it back to court and I was required to allow them conduct a home study with the county where we now lived. This was to let the county where the kids were being held know if I had a proper home. I had been seeing my kids on my days off work. This showed my case workers that I really was a loving mother. I deserved my kids back and the day we went to court, I was once again granted custody of Wade and Cory.

I was able to get my boys and bring them away from the bad influences of Moore County. Since I was no longer required to pay child support I would have more money to spend on them. They deserved it after all the hell they had been through during the past few years. I enrolled them into school and life could not have been more wonderful for me and my boys.

The year 2008 arrives and I am still living with John but I notice mine an John's relationship isn't what it once was. He let me know that he was no longer attracted to me but I would never have to leave him unless I wanted to.   My kids and I could live at one end of the mobile home and rent two bedrooms and one bathroom from him. In addition, I would have use of the common areas such as the kitchen, laundry and living room. I felt hurt at first but John and I just could no longer get along with each other.

I believe it may be due to our age difference as John was in his late sixties while I was in my late twenties. I also noticed John had an eye for a woman who lived around the corner from him. She was considered the neighborhood drunk and the neighborhood whore and would sleep with any man she could get her hands on provided he had a carton of beer. John loved this because I was not a drinker while and he and this woman loved drinking beer. At every opportunity they would get together and drink. He eventually became attracted to her.

As time passed and life continues, I tried to become more forgiving to the people who had hurt me. I learned to forgive my family for doing all the bad things they had done to me and to each other. Then 2009 came and my relationship with John had pretty much fallen apart. I began taking my paychecks and would wait for my kids to get home from school on Fridays and we would head to Ramseur in order to see my sisters and brothers. I would return on Sunday evening just in enough time to get the kids in bed for school the next day. I did this for quite a while.

I am now working a new job at the local Walmart because it paid me a little better. I also had house cleaning jobs I worked on my days off. This was to help me even more. One day I noticed Wade had red sores on his body and had to go to the doctor. He dug at his skin like he had fleas. Later, I discovered he had caught chicken pox. Walmart let me take a few days off work due to Wade being sick. The doctor told me that my other kids could catch this unless I was very careful. Sure enough, he was right. Winston soon contracted chicken pox.

Oh geese, this wasn't good. John and I both worked at Walmart and he helped watch the kids whenever he could. But, when I discovered Winston had chicken pox, it was about two days before I was told to be back to work following my absence due to Wade being sick. My manager told me if I did not return to work then he would have to let me go.

I lost my job but thankfully, I still had my cleaning jobs around town and at this point my cleaning jobs had grown quite well. I had more houses to clean because my customers would refer me to other people. This was great, as I needed a steady income. I was making a pretty good living by cleaning other peoples trash but the pay made it all worthwhile.

By April of 2009 I remember meeting a neighbor of mine who I had previously only seen in passing. Officially, until now, we had never met. One day while I was walking to the bus stop to get my children, up drives a white mustang. It was my neighbor from out back. He got out of his car and we shook hands to greet each other.

He introduced himself as Alfred Brown. I told him my name and he let me know I could visit him anytime I wanted. I let Alfred know I may just take him up on his offer someday. Mr. Brown got back into his mustang and drove away. I remember very well the exact thing Alfred was wearing that beautiful day. He was wearing a black shirt with white stripes, a pair of white jeans, black boots, a very nice black Stetson cowboy hat and the most wonderful, beautiful smile I have ever seen. I just felt like the sky had opened up and delivered an angel just for me. As time passed, he and I would have visits together at his house. This was OK since we were both single.

Alfred and I enjoyed every moment we were able to spend together. I began cleaning his house occasionally. Now, I believe Alfred never needed his house cleaned, he just knew I needed another dollar so he paid me for cleaning it. As time passed we became more and more intimate with each other. Every time I would come to visit, I hoped he would ask me to stay long term. This did not happen. Like any other single man Alfred did not want a long term relationship. Therefore, we kept things as they were for a while and we continued to spend time with each other.

When the boys were in school we'd have our free time alone. I just knew I was in love. I knew I had a nice thin body and figured that's all I needed to land Alfred. As it would turn out this was not to be the fact. I let no one know of my relationship with Alfred. The entire neighborhood would let me know of how Alfred Brown was a single man and they wanted him. My friend Shirly who lived a few houses up the road knew Alfred and she talked about him most everyday. This made me start to think differently of Alfred. Not in a bad way, just changing my feelings and if I was certain I needed to have a intimate relationship with him. It seemed all my neighbors, both men and woman were talking about him. When I would ask my neighbors they would let me know their thoughts about him. Alfred and I enjoyed all our time together and I didn't care what anyone else thought of us. We had very intimate moments whenever we were able to get together. He was so beautiful and I wanted him all to myself. And, I knew I would not stop at anything to land this man. He won my heart when I knew he loved my kids. As 2009 would draw to an end, I could not possibly prepare myself for what was about to happen next.

Chapter Six
Losing Bradly

Rumors spread throughout my family that my brother Bradly was a wanted man. Bradly was married with three small children all of which were under eleven years old. Bradly and his wife, Amy, were living in Dunbar, West Virginia. While living in Dunbar, he lived next door to a woman who had a young daughter named Missy. The two family's became close friends. Bradly and Amy began taking Missy to the park to play with their kids. As time passed and their friendship strengthened, they began doing more and more activities together. Eventually, there would be times when Bradly would take Missy off alone. For whatever reason, at age ten, Missy thought the sun rose and sat on Bradly. It did not matter to her that Bradly was a man around twenty-six years old. An intimate relationship started between them. This was awful!

Missy's mother was hooked on drugs and seemed not to give a damn where her daughter was or what she was doing. Her father was in prison after having been convicted of possession of child porn. None of our family knew anything other than the things Bradly told us about his now ten year old girlfriend.

Bradly left his wife in Dunbar, West Virginia and drove back to North Carolina to stay for awhile. Traveling back and forth between Ramseur and Dunbar to see Missy. Bradly and Missy believed they were in love. As things got worse, Amy, filed for a divorce and Bradly stayed away. Soon, Missy, who is now eleven, learns she is pregnant with Bradly's baby. When I found out, the first thing I thought was oh goodness how in the heck can something like this happen? My family knew that nothing good could come from this relationship.

When the State of West Virginia discovered Missy had gotten pregnant by a twenty-six year old man, they began a manhunt for my brother. Bradly was wanted for getting Missy pregnant and having sexual relations with an under age child. This soon turned out to be a nationwide manhunt. Bradly had already left the states of West Virginia and North Carolina and nobody in my family knew where he was living. We knew Missy was about due to have her baby. Somehow she and Bradly managed to talk while he was in hiding from the police. Although we did not know it at the time, we later we learned from Missy that Bradly had been living in Ohio.

Missy delivered a baby girl in March of 2006. This resulted in the investigation becoming even more sincere with the cops, the courts and the child support agency becoming more anxious to find him. They all wanted Bradly Ralph!

This would remain in the news for the next few years. Police were frequently calling my mother and asking for Bradly. The family still had no idea as to where Bradly was living. This was probably the first time in history my family managed to tell the truth. We all told the truth when asked his whereabouts by the cops. We were not hiding Bradly but he was hiding from the world. Bradly's picture was in the news on an almost daily basis throughout the State of West Virginia. Investigators in West Virginia were still calling my mother in North Carolina but we could not give answers to any of the questions they were asking. We just did not have a clue as to where Mr. Ralph was living or hiding.

Then November 2009 arrived and so did mom's birthday. After not having heard from him for years, he suddenly called mom. During his call to mom, Bradly let mom know he was the father of Missy's child and his plan to turn himself in to the state police in West Virginia. These were very serious charges that Bradly was facing, but he said that he was tired of hiding.

Bradly was permitted to date Missy with her mother's consent. This made Bradly think he would be in less trouble since Missy's mother had given them permission to date. She knew their age difference yet gave her permission. On December 31, 2009 Bradly turned himself in and was booked into the South Central Regional Jail facility. Bradly was ordered detained according to Kanawha County circuit court.

While in jail, he frequently called his sisters in North Carolina and let them know that he was fine. However, after a few days of jail life, he began complaining of pain in his stomach. The jail just gave him Tylenol and sent his back to his jail cell. As days went by January of 2010 arrives and the pain becomes even more unbearable.

The jail facility told him they could do lab work and see what was happening to cause his stomach pain. On January 5, 2010, his attorney went to court and ask for him to be transported to the local hospital. Her motion was denied by the judge. He told Bradly's attorney that he needed proof of blood work the jail could provide for the court. By now, Bradly was no longer in his cell but was instead in the nursing area of the jail. The nursing area still looked like a regular jail but he could be better monitored in this area.

Phone calls to my family had stopped. Bradly had been telling my sisters on the phone he hurt very badly. My sisters called the jail and requested that he be taken to the local hospital emergency room, but they were unsuccessful. On January 6, Bradly's blood work came back abnormal. With this information in hand, his attorney once again took the paperwork to the court and submitted a motion to have Bradly moved to the local emergency room. And again, the motion was denied. The judge told his attorney that he needed more proof in order to let Bradly go to a hospital. That proof needed to be a second opinion.

The attorney knew something was definitely wrong with Bradly but it was out of her hands. The judge called the shots on whether or not Bradly could be admitted to a hospital. His attorney went back to court on the 8th on his behalf but this time it was before a different judge. His attorney took one of the nurses from the jail with her in hopes it would allow the court to hear her opinion as to what could be causing the pain in Bradly's stomach. Because she was just a nurse and not hospital staff personnel, the motion was denied for a third time. The judge did agree that he could have a member of the hospital staff in the courtroom the following Monday morning. If they examined Bradly over the weekend they could get approval for him to be transported to the local hospital emergency room.

Knowing this was a big relief for my family. Bradly was too sick and could not speak for himself. the family had to be his mouth piece. This was a victory win for my family as they believed Bradly was strong enough to wait until Monday. Then he would get transported to the hospital. Bradly's cries and screams became very weak which made the jail staff think that maybe Bradly did need medical attention. But, they were ordered by the judge to not call for transportation to the hospital. As the pain worsened, he cried even more.

I truly believe that his attorney really did make every effort to help him. It was Sunday. The weekend was just about over and tomorrow he would finally get to a hospital. The nurses at the jail noticed his blood pressure was dropping. He would constantly vomit and continue to cry. My family was still talking with the jail staff in an effort to get more for help Bradly. At 5:52 PM the jail made the decision to keep a closer eye on him. They continued to hear him beg for help and crying in agony, but help never came.

Bradly finally stopped crying after days of crying and vomiting. The nurses thought he had finally just fell asleep and tried to rest. According to the jail staff, he had not slept in days. At 5:58 PM the staff came to check on Bradly. They found him unresponsive. He had no pulse so the staff called the ambulance. Bradly was pronounced dead at 6:08 PM on January 10, 2010.

When Bradly checked into the jail, he had given them the phone number and address of his new girlfriend who lived in Ohio. The jail called her and it was her father who, in turn, called mom to inform us that Bradly had died. Of course, this just about killed my mother. For once in my life I felt sorry for my mother.

I remember when I got the news that Bradly had died I was in Leland, North Carolina eating dinner at a Smithfield restaurant. My phone must have rang fifty or more times. It was my mother's house number. I didn't want to answer the phone. I did not want to talk to her as I did not agree with the way she and Luke lived so, I turned my phone off until I was finished eating dinner.

After dinner I turned on my phone. I had oh so many voice mails to call mom's house which I did.

When I called Luke Wayne answered the phone and told me something bad had happened. I heard a lot of noise and mom crying in the background. Then Luke told me that Bradly had passed away. This couldn't be true I thought. Bradly was a healthy twenty-nine year old man. Nobody, including the jail, at this point knew how he died. I cried so hard, I couldn't believe he had died, he was too young.

I went back to the home that John and I shared and he agreed to watch my boys so I could go to mom's house and find out just what the world was going on. So I did just that. It is a four hour drive to mom's place and I left as soon as I had packed me some clothes. Bradly's funeral would not be anytime soon as he was being transported to the medical examiners office in South Charleston, West Virginia for a autopsy. Evening came and I finally made it to mom's place where all the family were gathering. We could do nothing but wait for more information concerning Bradly from people in West Virginia. I stayed at mom's along with other family members to see if any news would come from Bradly's autopsy.

West Virginia did his autopsy on January the 12th. This was my sons birthday. I believe it is the first year Cory has not had a birthday bash with streamers and balloons. Even while in foster care I was permitted to spend their birthday with my kids.

This birthday for Cory was a sad one for me. I came home to see my kids and get ready to return in a few days for Bradly's funeral. Alfred Brown had baked Cory a birthday cake and bought him a few presents for his birthday. Cory understood that I was sad and didn't want to party for his birthday.

Now came the time we needed to find out how we were going to rake up enough money to bury Bradly. His body was in West Virginia. Mom wanted him to be buried here in North Carolina. This was impossible to do without money. My family didn't have bank accounts or have sufficient credit so getting a bank loan was impossible. It was going to cost an estimated $12,000 or more to bury him. This would include the cost of shipping his body from West Virginia to Ramseur, North Carolina.

Over the next few days we tried to come up with enough money to get his body shipped to Ramseur. My family agreed that since we lived in North Carolina that Bradly's burial should be here and not in Ohio where he was born.

As luck would have it, Tabitha was still dating Brad Samuels's old boss, Oliver Beckley. This is how my family was able to get the money to bury Bradly. Oliver provided every dollar of it in the form of a loan. Bradly used to work for Mr. Beckley at the same sawmill where Brad Samuels and Luke Wayne worked. Oliver, Tabitha and mom all went to the bank where Oliver cosigned the loan for mom. This was for the total amount the funeral home needed to transport Bradly's body from West Virginia and provide him a reasonably nice funeral. Now, Oliver didn't like my mother and Luke as he knew too well as to what they were all about, lies and corruption. However, Oliver Beckley was so much in love with Tabitha he would do anything for her.

During the next few days, Bradly's body made its way back to the Lofflin Funeral Home in Ramseur, North

Carolina. They called to let mom know Bradly's body had arrived. They requested that someone come to the funeral home to identify his body.

Mom couldn't do it! She wouldn't do it! Instead, mom sent Cindy, her husband Scott, Maranda, and Keith, Jr. in her place. Once they all got there, the funeral home personnel took them into a private room. Bradly's body was covered from head to toe with a white sheet. I was told by my siblings the funeral home staff proceeded to uncover Bradly's face. The sheet made it to Bradly's shoulders. They said Bradly did not look the same. Then they uncovered him down to the waist area revealing the cuts on his skin as the result of his autopsy. They positively identified him as being our brother Bradly. Although I wasn't there, I can imagine the feelings they must have had while viewing Bradly's body.

The family left and we began making arrangements for his funeral. Later in the evening mom received another phone call from the funeral home. This call was to let her know they had Bradly's clothes from West Virginia which had arrived along with his body.

Mom believed these were the same clothes he had worn when he first checked into jail on December 31, 2009. She was told to send someone to the funeral home to collect these belongings. It was my brother Keith, Jr. who went to the funeral home and collected the bag containing Bradly's belongings. The bag was sealed with tape and Keith, Jr. had no idea what was inside of the bag. He took the bag to mom's house where mom and all her kids were gathered.

All six of mom's children were standing around the kitchen table anxiously waiting for mom to open this bright orange bag that had traveled with Bradly's body all the way back from West Virginia. Like I stated earlier, we all believed that we was going to see Bradly's personal belongings that he had on him when he went into jail in December. Things such as clothes, keys and wallet. Mom had this orange bio chemical bag which was sealed with tape. Writing on the tape around it said "EVIDENCE" with Bradly's name printed on it. It had Bradly's name on white stickers with his date of birth and date of death. It was plainly identified as Bradly's bag.

Now came time to open it. Mom didn't want anybody but her to touch it. So we stood around the table watching as she opened the bag. She used a pair of scissors to cut the tape. Then, she slowly opened the bag. The odor coming out of the bag was terrible. Something I had never before smelled. It must have been the smell of death. That's the only way to put it. Mom reached inside and pulled out two white socks that were folded up inside each other. She laid them flat on the table for us to see. Then she pulled out a orange shirt. It was covered with vomit. We begged mom to stop looking at the items but she insisted so we let her continue. Next mom reached into the bag and pulled out a pair of orange pants. They were soiled with human waste. Mom cried more and more as she pulled the clothes closer to her chest. Bradly's white underwear was inside the pants. He must have had a bowel movement as the result of his muscles relaxing when he died. This caused human waste go all over mom's hands. We all agreed to take them from her at which time the house turned into a boxing ring or somewhat of a free for all.

We all tried to get the clothes out of mom's sight.

She had Bradly's stool, human waste, on her clothes, her arms and her hands. We all grabbed at mom's arms in an effort to take everything away from her. By the time mom and us kids had quit fighting, we were all covered with Bradly's last bowel movement along with other unidentifiable bodily fluids.

We all cried and cried. I couldn't believe this. This was the orange jump suit they had clothed Bradly in when he was first admitted to jail. Who's idea was it to send the contents of this bag to my mother in such a manner? It should have been destroyed. Bradly's body laid in those clothes and he used the bathroom in them. Is this what is suppose to happen when people pass away? I don't think it is normal to have kept these clothes. Instead, I believe they should have been destroyed.

Mother immediately contacted an attorney. One that would not require any money up front. She knew she had a law suit. The funeral home in Ramseur later explained to us at the funeral, that if they had known what was inside that bag they would have never brought it back with Bradly's body. They felt very badly for my mother as did everyone who has heard this story.

Mom's attorney came to North Carolina to begin the initial proceedings for her lawsuit. Eleven days after Bradly's death and the family still had not a clue as to how or why he died.

Mom had asked me to call her brother in Ohio and see if he knew how to find dad. Dad needed to know the stepson he had help to raise was dead. We had his funeral. The evening of Bradly's showing we headed to the funeral home.

Cindy, Keith, Jr. Vivian, and Maranda were the

ones in our immediate family who arrived first. I drove mom and we walked into the funeral home together. Once inside, the funeral director met us at the door. He let mom know that Bradly's body was lying in his casket on the other side of the wall. He told mom she should take her time. Mom was ready to get this over so she and I walked around the corner and saw Bradly's casket and then walked slowly toward it. As we reached the casket, mom tried touching it when she fell. She fell in the floor crying over Bradly.

The funeral home cleared our family from the room. We were the only people there because it was the family hour. Mom was taken to another room where she sat down and greeted people who came to mourn Bradly's death. Once we resumed the funeral visitation hours, I noticed that dad must have gotten the message that Bradly had passed away. I noticed the flowers he had sent while looking at everyone else's flowers. So the delivery of my message to him was successful. I was relieved. Dad later claimed he did not have money enough to travel to North Carolina to attend his son's funeral.

That evening I remember mom asking for the funeral home to find extra security for the service to be held tomorrow. This was because Bradly's ex wife, the mother of his three kids, along with the thirteen year old mother of one of his kids and his current girlfriend at time he passed away were going to be there. They complied with her request because just about every cop in Ramseur were there at the funeral. They also followed us to the cemetery. This was because my family and the mother's of his kids could not get along with each other. Somehow, we all made it through the funeral without fighting. Bradly was buried in a nice clean cemetery. Then life without our Bradly began.

Chapter Seven
A Very Bad Year

As 2010 was coming to an end, mom continued to meet with her attorney and things were beginning to change in all our lives. I was still living in Shallotte, North Carolina with my boys and John. I was back and forth between friends and John's house. By this time John had fallen for the married woman who lived a few doors from him. She is considered as the community drunk. And, I was so in love with Alfred I wanted to be with him constantly. I am taking life much more seriously than I did in the past. I now realize I wanted to settle down and get married. I just needed to find the perfect man. It seems in this world that a great man, a hard working man, is hard to find. In fact, almost impossible to find.

I discovered that my father in Ohio was talking once again to my mother here in North Carolina. I didn't understand why because mom always used the words, I hate your father Keith so much. But, as things would turn out, mom and dad got back together in October of 2010. Rumors began to spread that maybe dad was only getting back with mom for her lawsuit money over Bradly's death. The money wasn't here yet but it would definitely not be too much longer in arriving. Even I thought dad was back with mom for that reason and I wasn't the only one in the family to express these thoughts. Honestly, I think all of mom's children had that thought go through their heads.

Mom quickly dumped Luke Wayne and went to Ohio to get dad. When mom returned, she discovered that Luke had taken most of their belongings. He went back to his family who were living in New York. Later, prior to his death in 2015, we learned he was dating a woman named Joyce. My sister Cindy kept in touch with him until he passed away.

When mom and dad moved into the trailer she and Luke had shared, it was like a family reunion to my family. Dad had not seen any of his grandchildren except for Cory at the time he was born. It took time for dad to get to know his grandchildren. Cindy had one son, Maranda had five children, Vivian had two girls, Bradly had four children, I had five children and Tabitha had two girls. Keith, Jr. was the only one that has not yet had any children. That is, none that we know of. Dad had to get to know all these kids and they had to get to know dad.

My life wasn't so simple by this time. Social services had once again been receiving calls concerning me and my boys. I believe it was my sister and mother who were filing the false complaints. Mom was once again telling lies to my father and their relationship was going downhill at a fast pace.

I would never visit them like my brother and sisters did. Instead, I stayed to myself in Shallotte, about three hours away. My sisters seemed to find it necessary to show off their kids to dad while mine seemed to just be pushed aside. This upset me to the point it would almost make me sick. Once again, my boys were getting the shit end of the stick. But, I had become accustomed to it. Wade, Winston and Cory barely spent any time with dad and mom. And, they never stayed overnights with them. Everyone in my family says it is because I lived so far away. Mom's lawsuit became the center of attention for the entire family.

We now have received the results of Bradly's autopsy. It stated that he had died of paratinitous. This is a condition where holes had developed in his bowels. I believe there were about twenty-three holes in which the autopsy showed. Bradly hurt in his stomach due to his waste having leaked out through these holes. As a result it poisoned his body. When he was vomiting in jail, we were told, the vomit in his mouth was in reality human waste. The autopsy also determined Bradly had suffered heart failure due to the human waste leaking into his body raced to his heart killing him.

With the additional knowledge, the lawsuit was altered. We had proof that Bradly had not been faking while in jail when he begged and begged for the help that never arrived. Thus, the lawsuit was expanded further to include the jail. Had he received medical help when he asked for it, he would have lived. Mom was suing a couple of other organizations in West Virginia.

She was suing the jail, because when they did Bradly's blood work on January 5, 2010 but it was not submitted to his lawyer until much later. This resulted in more delay in getting help. She was also suing the judge who denied Bradly the right to emergency room treatment. She also was suing the county medical examiner's office because they sent the very clothes in which Bradly had died along with his body to the funeral home in North Carolina. Those clothes should have been burned. This was an enormous lawsuit for my mother. As the year 2010 came to an end and mom and dad were still trying to rekindle their old love. And, I began having more phone calls made to social services concerning me and the boys.

I really blame myself for what was about to happen next. You see, I had let everyone know how terrified I was concerning social services. I could not trust a soul.

Everyone of my friends and family knew that I was so afraid of social services. It was my fault for having let people close to me know my past. Seems everything I had ever told anyone would somehow be used against me. The new county to which I had moved were now getting calls concerning me. I had been living here almost four years and the complaints did quit for awhile. But out of the blue, they have now started back up again.

My family is so evil. I discovered later, through my attorneys, they were the ones making the calls to social services. My mother is just the type of person to do such a thing. Mom knew all of her children except Keith, Jr. had children. She would constantly ask all of us to give her money to help pay her living expenses because her disability check was never enough.

Whenever we did not give her the money she thought we should, or didn't cater to her every demand, she would call us children names like; mother fuckers, bitches, bastards, whores, sluts, or she would refer to us as my mother fucking little bastards. To be truthful, I have heard her say such things to Bradly as well. Mom has a way of staying mad at us when she didn't get her way. She was like a spoiled brat in a candy store. If she didn't get something she would pitch a fit. That's what mom did then and still does to this day.

The calls made to social services accused me of doing bad things to my kids. I'll not go into detail as I could write forever concerning the things they would falsely accuse me of doing. I will say that it wasn't just my mother that had called the department of social services. As it turned out there was a handful of people whom I trusted very much that had made the calls.

During the next few months I began to realize that my son Winston was having problems. At three and a half years old he began to have bleeding incidents without injuries. Seems everywhere we went he was having nose bleeds. It mattered not where or what we were doing he would have a nose bleed. I took Winston to the local emergency room and they just said he had most probably picked his nose causing it to bleed. I came home from the hospital and he continued to bleed. It wasn't just an ordinary nose bleed. There were enormous amounts of blood.

I knew that something was not right so I took him to a different emergency room. And, they tell me the same thing. Winston was a healthy baby and I should buy him some mittens to put on his hands so he cannot pick his nose. I took Winston home cried at the fact for I knew he was sick. I needed a doctor who would agree with me. This continued for a while, and I took him to other emergency rooms hoping for an answer. They too, like the others, would send us home. Winston was normal, so I waited for him to bleed again. Experience told me that whenever he would bleed, it would last at least twenty minutes.

Then, I drove Winston to a hospital in Myrtle Beach, South Carolina which is about forty miles from Shallotte. The other three hospitals where I had taken him to thought I was crazy. They thought Winston could not have bled as much as I had told them.

We arrived at the hospital in Myrtle Beach and I let them know Winston had bled so much over the past little while and that his nose was full of dried blood clots. He was breathing and eating through his mouth. Upon finding nothing wrong with Winston I finally got a referral for a local ENT doctor to look at him. I was excited. Winston was going to get help in two days.

I went to the ENT appointment as scheduled. The doctor told me his nose was blocked off because of bleeding. He needed it cleaned out and he needed his tonsils taken out due to him breathing and eating through his mouth.

He was scheduled for immediate surgery. I went to the hospital to get his labs done as the ENT had requested and we now had a surgery scheduled for the next morning. Winston was finally going to get help. Or, so I thought. The ENT doctor asked me to come in very quickly. When I arrived, I was told the surgery had been canceled. I asked why and was told Winston's blood work did not look good.

The doctor asks if I could be at the hospital in Chapel Hill, North Carolina the next morning and I told him that I could. I was given an appointment to see the hemophilia team for children. This was a cancer and blood doctor. I left the hospital in South Carolina and went home where I packed my bags. My boys and I drove the four hours that night to a hotel in Chapel Hill. The next morning I was at the hospital in Chapel Hill.

The doctors examined Winston and while I repeated to them what his symptoms were. They did blood work and put me in a room without my kids while another person took Wade and Cory to look at the toys they had in their waiting room. I sat patiently waiting for news about my Winston. I knew if something was wrong with him, this hospital was capable of finding his problem. I knew of their reputation as people from all over the world would come to this hospital for treatment.

The team of doctors came in a little later and delivered some bad news to me. We discussed the situation where no one would believe me whenever I told them how badly Winston would bleed. The doctor looked me in the eye and let me know that he believed me. He said he had some news for me but I did not need to start crying until I heard him out. I said OK.

He proceeded to tell me that he believes Winston had one of two things. He said the only thing that would make you bleed as much as Winston had been doing, is leukemia or another blood disease. He also told me that Winston did need his tonsils removed as well as a nose cauterize. He added that the blood work needed to come back before they could do any surgery. He said the blood work can take anywhere from a few hours up to as much as twelve days.

I could not help but fall apart. He told me I should go home and wait for a phone call from him. After crying about two hours in the hospital lounge, I settled down and headed back home. My three children had no idea as to what was going on. I had not slept in hours for I was too worried about Winston. I had only been driving about a hour when my cell phone rang. It was the Chapel Hill hospital so I pulled the car over at the next place I could get off the road and so I could hear every word of the doctors were saying about Winston's test results.

They told the great news was he did not have leukemia. I was so relieved. They told me that he did have another type of blood disease and the name for the disease is Von Willebrand Disease. I began crying again. It seems all I could do was cry. As a mother I was suppose to protect my children but I am hopeless. I cannot fix this problem.

The doctor let me know that I should return to the hospital immediately. Winston needed blood and both his tonsils and his adenoids needed to be taken out. He asked if could I return tomorrow and I told him that I could. He told me I could check into the hospital tomorrow and Winston would have surgery his surgery the following morning. He knew that I was heading home and needed to get our clothes together and then I would return.

So, it was set in stone, my baby was not born healthy as they had told me the day when he was born. I returned home to prepare for my trip back to the hospital. I packed more clean clothes for Winston and me.

Wade and Cory had to be in school so I made arrangement for them to stay with friends. Winston and I drove back to the hospital in Chapel Hill. All the while, the thoughts going through my mind about how I was told he was born a healthy child. When I ask the doctors at the hospital how Winston had gotten this disease, they stated that was genetic. That it had been passed down to Winston from either me or his father.

We arrived at the children's hospital that evening and Winston was admitted and given a room. I was greeted by the same doctor I had seen earlier. He provided me with more information than when we spoke on the phone. The night passed but I did not get any sleep. I was much to worried about Winston's surgery to get any sleep. It was 4:00 AM, when the doctors and hospital staff took Winston to the operating room for his first surgery.

The surgery was successful and Winston made it through the operation. They removed both his tonsils and his adenoids. They cauterized his nose and made him an artificial clot so as to catch more blood should he have any future bleeds. Nose bleeds are a common occurrence when you have Von Willesbrands Disease and you can bleed without having an injury.

Winston had been born without factor 8. It is factor 8 that helps the body produce blood platelets needed to help with blood clotting. As time passed we had to make adjustments to our lives as Winston would always have this problem. As far as I am concerned, he is still perfect and I would not trade him for anything.

Mom's lawsuit was in and out of court however they had not yet settled anything. At every court date we children would try to go with her to West Virginia and attend the court hearings with her. As time passed I would manage in someway to cause someone to be upset with me. As a result, I would have social services on my doorstep the following day. It seemed to be a toss up for me. Either Winston having problems with this blood disease which is the worst part of my life. Or, I had to always wonder if social services was going to visit me because I had pissed off someone. In addition, my social life was not so good either. I was seeing Alfred occasionally but not as much as I wanted. I struggled constantly to just keep my head afloat and not drown in all of life's problems. Knowing full well that if I managed to make my mother upset at me, I would have my workers at my door wanting to open another case. I knew most of this was my mother's work at best.

Eventually I moved out from John's house and moved in with my close friend Samatha. Her husband had recently left her and her kids and as a result she, like me, needed some help. My kids and I moved in with her and rented a room from her. Her kids shared a room and, I shared the room I rented with my boys. While there I made sure my boys had everything they needed. During the time we lived with Samantha social service visits slowed for a bit and almost stopped altogether. I was finally getting cut some slack.

I soon realized that I had become a built in babysitter for Samatha. She had recently returned to living the single life and partied while I stayed home with both my kids and hers. Samatha was using me and I got fed up with it.

I realized that I needed to leave and, I wanted to leave state but because of my open cases with social services I could not leave the state permanently. I crawled back to Alfred Brown for help like the many times before. He had spent thousands of dollars to help me pay the fees necessary to hire the attorneys I needed to represent me so I could keep my children. Oh how I wanted so badly to leave the state and run away to a place where nobody knew me. But, I could not due to the many open cases with social services. I found myself in trouble and trying to save my kids without an attorney was impossible.

I'll try and give an example. Someone could call social services and say I was beating and starving my kids. Social services had to investigate every call that was made concerning me. And, when they opened a case, it remained open for quite a while. And yes, every time I made some one upset at me, as I frequently did, I had workers at my door the following day. Both my family and my closest friends knew very well that my kids were my world. They knew how much I cried whenever a new case was opened. Although there was never any proof of abuse, there was still a chance of loosing the kids due to past cases in Moore County that had occurred prior to Winston being born.

I had been asked to give up the rights to my three boys on a number of occasions. Social services suggested that I should voluntarily give them custody of the kids so that I would not have to fight anymore. My answer to them was, "it would be a cold very cold day in hell before I turned my kids over to the state of North Carolina". They brought it up in court that I had given up a child in the year 2001 through a legal adoption. Evidentially, this was in hopes the judge would be on their side and grant them custody.

The judge asked me if I wanted to keep my boys and I answered, yes sir. This was the end to them questioning me about signing my boys over to them. They knew if they tried to take my kids, they would have to fight me for them.

During years 2011 and 2012 Winston continued to have more surgeries. He was constantly in and out of the hospital at Chapel Hill. And during this time visits with my mom and dad were very few. We received word that in December of 2012 final settlement for mom's lawsuit concerning Bradly would be concluded. We felt that it wasn't about the money, it was about getting justice for what had happened to Bradly.

I cannot speak for the rest of my family, but that is the way I saw it. Mom had been borrowing money from anyone and everyone she could. She kept a little notebook detailing what she owed to everyone. Yes, she owed me money too. She promised she would repay everyone when her settlement came through. Whenever mom needed anything like food, she made sure someone would lend her the money for her needs. She had a smoking habit and would smoke about five packs of cigarettes a day and dad seem to be doing about the same. There was no way I could afford to keep them in cigarettes. I would wire them money whenever I could. Should I fail, you can only guess, I had social service workers knocking on my door. I busted my butt working at cleaning houses to support both my kids and other family members.

November came of that year and I heard all my family had gotten their summons to be in court in West Virginia concerning mom's settlement. I was the last one in the family to receive mine. I really didn't want to go drive to West Virginia on the court date but I was ordered by the court to be in attendance. The date finally arrived and we were all there.

We were notified by mail the hearing would be closed and that neither children or the public would be allowed inside the courtroom. As mom and we kids entered the courtroom to put an end to it all, I was relieved it was almost over. Mom deserved closure.

Dad stayed behind in North Carolina while mom and we children attended the settlement hearing. During the hearing the judge only permitted us to be in the room. The people my mother was suing were there along with their lawyers. The mother's of Bradly's children thought they would be allowed inside the courtroom but they were prohibited from attending. This was a private hearing open only to mom's immediate family. The judge made sure that Bradly's family received justice.

The lawsuit was settled between mom and the

three parties she was suing. In doing so, each one of mom's children were asked to stand and state to the court their name, age, and why they thought mom deserved the settlement. When my turn came to talk, I stated my name and age as I was requested to do. I was asked to state why I believed the case should be settled for this amount of money. I said what was on my mind. I said Bradly would have lived if he had received medical attention. That he was only twenty-nine years old, one year older than me. I added that mom should not have had to bury a child. Further, I could not understand why they could not have handcuffed him to a bed and taken him to a hospital for proper evaluation and treatment.

After talking to the judge, I began crying. I tried not to cry but it just happened. I had watched my mother sit through just about all of the court dates and now it was finally over. Case closed! And, mom walked away with a huge sum of money. As was agreed in the settlement, no one is allowed to disclose the actual amount of the settlement. We all headed back to North Carolina and all were glad her case concerning Bradly's wrongful death was finally over. I think it only lacked a few days of being three years since his death. It is finally over.

Chapter Eight
Saying Goodbye

It is now 2013 and like most people who come into a lot of unexpected cash, dad and mom were spending the money they received from Bradly's lawsuit like it was going out of style. I find that when people who have never had much money and are not use to managing money soon find it runs like water through their fingers. All mom's kids seemed to begin having emergencies and needed her cash to take care of them. Mom gave Vivian the money she needed to install a new roof for her house. And then she needed more money to remodel the inside of it.

Tabitha and her two girls moved in with mom, so that she could take care of all their financial needs.

Keith, Jr. was released from jail after mom paid all of his fines. Additionally, once he was released, he also moved in with her.

Cindy and Scott needed financial help. Everyone began to ask mom to repay every cent she and ever borrowed from them. I did ask for my money back but I never received an answer as to why she would not repay me for any of the money I had given her. It seemed each of them were living in a trailer park by now and could not get enough money from mom to satisfy all their wants and needs. I played it safe and just stayed clear of them all. The boys and I never received phone calls or letters from her like her other grandchildren did.

Yes, you would be correct if you said I was jealous. Mom and dad had already moved in with each other but they were trying to find a more desirable house to buy. The trailer in which they were living had most all of their belongings boxed up and ready for moving. They had only kept out a few necessities. As January and February came and went and then March arrived mom and dad were still looking and planning to move.

Cindy and Scott's son, the one who was born with difficulties, got sick. Cindy drove him to the Chatham hospital in Siler City. From there, he was then airlifted to Chapel Hill hospital in Durham, North Carolina. He had kidney failure. While leaving dad at home, mom and Keith Jr. went to the Chapel Hill hospital. Her grandson, Payton, was on the verge of death. In addition to his kidney problem, he has a condition called Williams Syndrome.

Mom and Keith Jr. stayed the night and drove home the next morning. When they arrived home, dad told mom that he had not slept any during the night. They were all tired from lack of sleep so they went to bed to get some rest. I remember trying to call mom throughout the morning in order to get an update of my nephew's condition. Nobody answered the phone.

It was Friday the fifteenth. I remember not hearing a thing all morning. Then, my phone finally rang. It was my mother, and she said, "get here quick, he has stopped breathing!"

Naturally, I believed my nephew had stopped breathing. I drove straight to the middle school to get Cory. Afterwards, while not having any other calls, I drove to the elementary school to pick up Wade. I left my phone in the car with Cory while I went inside the school to pick up Wade. When Wade and I returned, Cory told me my sister had called. My efforts to return her call were unsuccessful. I left a message on her voicemail to return my call. I left the school and had driven less than a half mile when brother Keith, Jr. called. I said hello, what's going on?

He told me dad had just dropped dead! He told me that dad was wearing his pajamas and walked into the bedroom to get into his everyday clothes. Mom heard something fall. She thought perhaps dad had dropped one of the boxes they had packed that had been stored in their bedroom. She walked into the room a few minutes later and found dad lying face down on the floor. He wasn't dead but she could tell he was having a medical emergency.

Tabitha called 911 and the operator asks my sister and brother to perform CPR on dad. They were both doing CPR on dad and continued until the EMT personnel arrived in the ambulance. Once they arrived, they took over and struggled to revive dad. They took needles and shot something into his heart in an effort to revive him.

While removing dad from the house, they used the side door in the kitchen. They felt it was easier to get dad through this door. However while going around the corner with dad's body, they cut his arm severely on the door facing. Blood went everywhere. They began their trip to the hospital with Tabitha, Keith Jr. and mom following closely behind the ambulance.

When they arrived at the hospital they made the family sit in a special waiting room. The hospital staff worked and worked on dad in an effort to save his life but they were unsuccessful. Dad was pronounced dead shortly after arriving at the hospital. The hospital staff allowed mom, Tabitha and Keith, Jr. see dad's body. When they entered they said that he had tubes all over his body from where they had been working on him. After a brief period of time they were asked to leave and life now begins without dad.

When I got the news that dad had died, I packed my bags and drove to Ramseur. When I arrived at mom's place, she and everyone else in the house were crying. Later that evening Keith, Jr. along with Vivian and Tabitha had to clean up the mess that was created during dad's death. There was blood on the floor beside the bed where dad had fallen. The area was littered with used rubber gloves, needle caps, and other papers that were used by the EMT workers. We worked half the night to remove blood from the bedroom and hallway floors.

Soon it was time to decide where we would bury daddy. Unlike when Brian passed away and we didn't have money to bury him, this time mom had money from the lawsuit to bury dad. A small portion of the family decided dad should be buried in West Virginia. Mom's father along with many of her other ancestors were buried there at the Maher cemetery. And, she always said she would want to be buried there as well. I did not, in any way, want him buried there. But, I wasn't allowed to be included into the decision making process. Seems I was always brushed aside like a pile of trash.

Dad's body was shipped to West Virginia and we had his funeral there. Tabitha, Keith Jr., Vivian, and mom were the only ones who had any say concerning dad's funeral. Mom quickly let everyone know that Maranda was not allowed to attend dad's funeral. Cindy could not attend the funeral as she was at the hospital in Chapel Hill, North Carolina with her sick son. That only left me, Tabitha, Keith Jr., Vivian, and mom. Mom told us that if we did not agree with her as to where to bury dad, then she would not pay for his funeral.

When mom and the other kids went into the funeral

home to make the funeral arrangements, I was told to sit outside in my car. I did not need to attend the meeting at the funeral home. This was hurtful for me because, as far as I was concerned, I was a Kendal too. Vivian was not one of dad's biological children. And, mom and dad had been divorced for years. I felt that I had more of a right to be in the meeting than either mom or Vivian. This started a argument between them and me. I separated myself from mom and my siblings. I even thought about driving back to North Carolina and miss my dad's funeral altogether.

Instead, I figured that I would just go rent a motel room. And, so I did just that. When I checked into the hotel room the snow began to fall more and more. Later, my kids and I heard a knock at the motel door. It was brother Keith. I wondered, how did he know I was here? I was extremely upset with them. I really wanted to leave that night but I knew if I did, I would regret it for the rest of my life. Keith had seen my car in the parking lot of the hotel and he knew I was there. To make a long story short, I had to put up with drama half the night. They had all shared a room but my kids and I had one of our own.

Soon the funeral was over and dad was buried in a nice cemetery. It snowed throughout dad's funeral. It snowed even worse, while driving approximately thirty miles from the funeral home to the cemetery. It was a very cold March day when we left dad behind and begin or drive back to North Carolina. I just couldn't believe dad was gone. When I read dad's obituary, I was shocked to see that Maranda's name had been omitted. This was both terrible and deliberate! My mother treated her family members like shit! But, this time things went too far. I know Maranda, to this very day, will probably never forgive mom for such an unforgivable act. I know I would not be able to forgive her if she had done something like this to me.

The drive from West Virginia to North Carolina was a long one. Normally it is about a nine hour trip but it seemed longer this time. We finally arrived home to Shallotte, North Carolina.

At this time I was living with a man named Matt, whom I had already determined I could no longer get along with. His family always tried to make me feel they were better than me. I knew this is not a situation where I wanted to be. By June of 2013 I let all my friends know that I needed to find a place to rent. I could no longer bare to so much as look at a man who thought he was better than me. And, he did not like the fact that I had to constantly stay nights, long nights, away at the hospital in Chapel Hill with my sick child. I was finished with Matt. All I needed to do is find a place to rent. I knew that I did not want to run back to my family, and even if they gave me a choice to do so, I would not return to live with them.

My mother was spending what money she had left from Bradly's lawsuit. She was nearly broke and had nothing to show for any of the money she had received. By this time mom was the mother of six children and the grandmother of nineteen. And, she was once again without a man. Tabnitha and Keith, Jr. were still living with her. Vivian is still married and living in Wagram, NC. Cindy along with her husband and child were living in the same old trailer that mom and Luke Wayne had once lived in. Maranda and her kids were living in South Carolina.

I, on the other hand, was living at Shallotte and I was looking for love. I had been betrayed by everyone who's path I had ever crossed. I wanted my children to grow up in better family environment than I did. I wanted them to attend and finish school. I wanted them to have the childhood that I was never able to have. My children deserved to live like a normal child. I wanted my children to know how lucky they were to just have tooth brushes. These are all the things I never had. I prayed and prayed I would find someone who loved me and my kids.

Chapter Nine
An Angel Appears

After all the rumors among my friends about me leaving, I finally got a break. My ex boyfriend, John, let me know he would talk with Mr. Alfred Brown and find out if he had any places to rent. I had not spoken to Alfred in a while. I wasn't sure he would rent me a place. Two days later, John let me know that he had spoken with Alfred and he told John that I could rent the mobile home next door to this house.

It is a small two bedroom mobile home with a living room and third bedroom addition. It had previously been used as a vacation place for the family that Alfred had bought it from. Alfred purchased the property at the time it was for sale in order to prevent anyone else from living too close to him. There is only about ten feet between his house and the mobile home. I decided to give Alfred a call and talk with him about renting the place to me.

I knew that I would take this deal because I could not stand living where I was very much longer. I packed our clothes and we moved into the mobile home next door to his house. Alfred would not accept rent from me. Instead, he allowed me to stay in his place rent free until I could find something better. I was happy to be where I was.

At this point I was receiving child support for Winston and Wade, but it was not steady or reliable as it was only every now and then that I would receive it. I moved into the Brown property on November 22, 2013. At this time, Alfred and I were both single. From the very night I moved in next door we spent every night with each other. Sometimes in the mobile home and sometimes at his house. As the month passed it was getting close to Christmas.

He let me know he would buy gifts for the kids this Christmas. This made me feel great as I did not have anything for them. Alfred let me know it would be OK if I moved into his house. It is a much bigger place than the one we were staying in. He told how he loved me and the boys. So I made my move into his beautiful home.

This started a war between me and few of his friends down the street. They could not stand me anymore than I could stand them. As the months passed and January turned into February. Alfred and I often had discussions about us getting married. You see, a few years ago when Alfred and I previously dated, we had spoken about getting married.

The day before Valentine's day of 2014, Alfred and I visited a local jewelry store where he bought my engagement ring as well as the wedding rings we would need when we get married. We soon announced our wedding plans to all of our family and friends. Alfred told me that I could pick any day I wanted for our wedding date as long as it wasn't a date already taken by some other special family event such as birthdays and anniversaries. The first date that popped into my mind was the month April. I chose April because I remembered it was the month of April that I had first met him.

Finally, we set the exact date to get married. It was set for April 4, 2014. I let Alfred know I wanted the ceremony to be held at the Brown house and that I did not need or want anything fancy. Just a simple wedding ceremony is all I wanted. On the day of our marriage, I began preparing the house and grounds very early in the morning. I had kept Cory out of school to assist me but I sent Wade and Winston to school as usual. Cory, Alfred and I were at home getting things ready for the service that was scheduled later in the evening. Since we was getting married at the house, we needed to get everything thing in perfect order.

While I was cleaning the living room windows, I noticed policemen from the Brunswick County sheriff department and a large number of narcotic's personnel were at the house directly across the street. I had previously heard the people living in the house were heavily involved in drugs. I considered them to be the trash of the neighborhood. I say this because they were trafficking in drugs while having small children living in their home. I quickly yelled for Alfred so he too could witness the drug raid in full bloom. There were policemen everywhere. Some were armed with assault rifles and stood guard along side the street. Finally the neighborhood trash was being taken out. But, it was being taken out in handcuffs by policemen instead of the local garbage service.

As the remainder of the day continued, family and friends arrived to attend our 6:00 O'clock PM wedding ceremony. We gathered around the bottom step of our front porch while the preacher stood on the top step and our guests were seated at table and chairs directly behind us.

As the preacher began our ceremony, he called me by the wrong name! He mistakenly called me Natalie! We heard the astonished reaction of our guests and someone even laughed out loud. It was a little accident, but it is still considered a big funny to this very day. Alfred says the preacher tried to change both my first and my last name. I still laugh whenever I think of it. I am not sure how he was able to get Natalie from Lilly and I didn't care. He could call me whatever he wanted so long as I was married to Alfred. The only thing that mattered to me by this time was me becoming Mrs. Brown. And, by 6:04 PM on April 4, 2014 we were Mr. & Mrs. Alfred D. Brown.

I was thirty-two years old and Alfred was seventy. We didn't care one bit if and when people talked about our age. We have never cared about our age difference one little bit.

The days following our marriage, I noticed the trash across the street was out of jail. They had posted bond and the drug house was soon up and running again. I cannot for the life of me understand how someone such as them get by with so much illegal drug activity in their lives. In addition to four adults, they also had five children living in the home. All I could think of was my past experiences with social services. People causing case after case to be opened on me while I was never on any type of drugs or alcohol. The family across the street proudly admits they love drugs and they still manage to keep their kids.

As my life continues our marriage has been nothing but sweet bliss. Alfred and I spend all our time together and enjoy every moment of it to the fullest. Even though there is a big age difference, we are so much in love and love living with each other. I have never loved anyone as much as I love my Alfred. Our marriage is a very wonderful thing. Alfred has taught me a lot since our marriage. My husband knows I have a difficult time reading and writing large words, and has helped me to improve my math skills along the way. While I am on the subject of my Alfred, let me just tell you a few things about him.

My Alfred, having served four years in the military during the nineteen sixties, is a U.S. Navy veteran. He has either worked as an electrician or taught electricity all of his adult live. He worked more that ten years with a public electrical utility company in West Virginia as a lineman, serviceman and meter man. He is a certified Master Electrician in the state of West Virginia and holds a Master of Science Degree from a major university in West Virginia. He is a licensed airplane pilot, and has many certifications within the mining industry for the states of West Virginia and Kentucky and the U.S. Mine Safety and Health Administration. Some of his certifications include Electrical instructor, Surface and Underground Mine Forman, and Explosive and Blasting instructor, Dust & Noise Sampling & Calibration, and Impoundment Inspector.

Alfred has owned and operated several business in the construction industry such as heating and air conditioning, sheet metal and roofing and a private training company. He is a retired school teacher with the state of West Virginia having taught in elementary, middle school, high school and college. He is also retired from a major coal mining company.

In addition to the above qualifications, Alfred has written and published three books, he plays the guitar, banjo, mandolin and keyboard. He owns the copyright for the many songs that he has written. Alfred is a very wonderful man. He is a man full of accomplishments. None which he will seldom mention or brag about.

Chapter Ten
Our Present Life

As the story of my life approaches the present time, I will end with an update on my family member's current situation. Sister Cindy, her husband Scott and their only child lives in a trailer that mom lived in many years ago with Luke Wayne. Cindy is a stay-at-home mom while Scott is currently employed as a school bus driver with the local school district. I have been told he often takes various recreational drugs in order to get high. Having little or no education Cindy struggles to live day to day. Or, as one may put it, she simply lives paycheck to paycheck. Their meager income is only enough for them to just barely get by.

My sister Maranda who have had several marriages and divorces now has five children and is married to a another woman named Lilly. None of my family ever knew Maranda was gay until a year ago. And nobody in my family likes the fact that she is gay. She currently lives in South Carolina and does not work, but her husband or wife does. When mom discovered Maranda was gay, she disowned her. Neither Maranda nor her partner Lilly has ever come to visit the family here in North Carolina. I love Maranda dearly and speak to her almost daily. I realize I cannot change the fact that she is gay.

Regardless, I still love her. Being a true believer of the Bible, I strongly believe that marriage is between one woman and one man. But, if Maranda believes differently and believes she is in love, then let her believe and do as she wishes. I fully understand that what is permitted by God's law and man's law are different. It did bother me for a few weeks after I had discovered she was gay. But I am fine with it now. To this day, I have never met my brother-in-law or sister-in-law, Lilly, which ever the case may be. I think it is a weird coincidence that we both have the same name. Even more weird is we both have a child whose name is Cory. She has a daughter and mine is a son. In any event, I wish them both the best of luck.

Vivian and her husband Randy along with their two daughters live in a nice, new, mobile home located at Wagram, NC. They have recently had their old home moved out and replaced by a new one. It is very nice but they are now stuck with making large house payments for many years to come. For, they only own the land while the bank owns the home. I have come to understand Randy smokes weed and is somewhat considered to be a pot head. Vivian used to smoke weed but I believe she has quit. Her health has declined since she has been married and she has had a few surgeries. She still has the bad habit of smoking cigarettes. Except for me, smoking cigarettes is a habit my entire family has. Perhaps, but not likely, one day they will quit.

Keith, Jr. lives in a small cabin located in Siler City, North Carolina. This is a small community about ten minutes from Cindy. He seems content with living the single lifestyle of a bachelor and dating any and every woman he is able to find. Keith has changed some as he has grown older. He has spent a few years in jail for having done some bad things, too many for me to talk about. He seems to have straightened up a lot but I have been told that he, like my other family members, also does drugs.

Tabitha has two girls from previous relationships. She has had a problem with diabetes since she was thirteen years old. She very recently married a man named Brandon. He has a severe alcoholic addiction.

Recently, Tabitha was approved for the disability for which she had applied and was awarded a large sum of money as a back payment. I was told that it was over forty thousand dollars. She bought a new mobile home and had it delivered and set up on property that belonged to Brandon's mother.

Things were going great with them until she decided she could not change her new husband's drinking habits. Each time he gets drunk and they have disagreements, Brandon asks her to leave the home she bought from the disability settlement. The cops have been called to her house on many occasions due to their frequent fighting. I have come to know they are both involved in drugs. Tabitha's drugs are the prescription drugs which the doctors prescribe for her pain. Brandon's drugs are recreational drugs as well as beer. Both he and Tabitha abuse drugs much too often.

As a result, their daughters, my two nieces, are caught in the middle of their wars. Since Brandon is frequently asking her to leave, her kids do not have a stable home environment. Although she and her family have visited me on occasion, I have never visited Tabitha at her home. And, it is probably better that I don't. Mostly, I have watched my nieces and nephews grow up through pictures. This is a method for me to keep abreast of my family while maintaining some distance between me and them.

My mother, on the other hand, is a completely different story. After dad passed, mom started dating a man named Ralph. While he adores my mother, I believe she feels completely different about him. You see, mom always thinks that she must be the head of the household.

She believes she can make any rule she desires and that the rule is then set in stone.

Mom has come to visit me and once here, she would ask that I lie to her boyfriend about why and how long she had visited. I let mom no, that I am not going to lie for her. It is for this reason, mom seldom visits me. She has a new man who lives near Raleigh, North Carolina. She slips away to see him whenever she can provided she can drum up an excuse to tell Ralph. When she is away spending a week or so there with the new guy, she tells Ralph she is here visiting her daughter and family. I feel sorry for Ralph as he has no idea that mom is playing both the fiddle and the harp.

She has a way of saying what's on her mind, however blunt or hurtful it may be. Recently I spoke to my husband about how each time I speak to mom on the phone, she uses the words like "MY CHILDREN MAKE ME SICK", or "MY BASTARD CHILDREN CAN GO TO HELL."

It makes me cry when she talks like this to me. She would also refer to us children as "BASTARDS AND BITCHES". What kind of mother says such things about her children? Especially after having had to bury one of them. How could she say something like that to her remaining children? I know my mother is taking pain pills in order to get high. Like the rest of my family, she too is on drugs. I've been told many of times by my mother "MY CHILDREN CAN BURN IN HELL". I could never imagine saying anything like that to my kids. My wonderful husband would witness how I would cry whenever mom spoke to me like this. He told me the next time mom called me a bad word, I should kindly say to her..... please don't talk like that to me. Sure enough having this in mind, mom called again, this time as soon as I said hello, she started cursing at me like I was a dog. After she had said what she wanted to say, I told mom to please not ever speak like that to me again. I told her that she hurt me every time I heard from her. She hung up on me and this is the last time I have spoken with her. I have not spoken to mom in several months but I still remember the time she called and referred to me and her other kids as "MOTHER FUCKERS, BITCHES AND BASTARDS". I guess that it was worth listening to her vulgar language during that last conversation, just to put an end to the evil in which my mother has injected into my life. She let all of her kids know that whoever has anything more to do with my gay sister, they cannot have anything to do with her.

For now, it looks like I am about finished with my corrupt mother. However, I do want to state that I most certainly do love my mom and my siblings. But, this does not mean that I will lie for them. And, I will not allow the drugs they use around me or my children. I know I am not a perfect person and I do not pretend to be one. However, I do believe to be living a better life than my siblings and mother. I have never used drugs of any kind and will not be a part of the selling of pills to each other like they often do.

I discovered they sell pills a while back when mother had visited me. I walked out onto my front porch and listened to a conversation she and my brother were having. It concerned selling pills when they returned home. I am so very sick of all the drugs that are in the world today. And, I am so grateful I don't have the desire to do drugs or smoke. It seems most of my entire family is a bunch of crooks.

Now that I have spoken about the living family members, let me speak about the deceased. Bradley's grave is always visited. My siblings frequently visits his grave and have kept it decorated with flowers. But, as to dad's grave, it is very sad.

My siblings had put a tombstone on his grave in West Virginia but the cemetery had it removed a week later. It was removed because it did not meet their requirements. So daddy is what I call, "THE MAN WITH NO NAME".

He is buried in the same cemetery as my grandpa, mom's dad, and the same cemetery in which my husband's first wife is buried. My husband will also be buried there at sometime in the future. The cemetery, Mountain View Memorial Gardens, is located at Maher, West Virginia on a narrow and winding section of land between Tug River and U. S. Highway 52.

I am told that mom had wanted to be buried there but she has recently changed her mind. I have often thought, why bury daddy there if mom was not planning to be buried there alongside him?

Now that I am thinking about it, maybe it is best that mom doesn't get buried there. After having treated my father the way she done. I feel a bit of relief she changed her mind. Mom is just mom and I believe she never will change.

On a different note, I am married to the most wonderful man in the world. His family is so much different than mine. His family does not try to hurt the other person like mine does. Instead, they are always trying to help each other in any way possible. I could not have asked for a better man.

I dearly love each and every one of Alfred's family. It has taken some time for my husband to know his mother-in-law. I think he has now learned exactly how she is. Actually, I know that he now knows her. I've had a wonderful past few years with my husband. My children and I never has to want for anything. Whenever the kids need something, Alfred buys them everything they need and much of anything they want.

Although I have a court order requiring Brad to pay child support for the boys, I am no longer receiving anything from him.. There is currently, an active warrant for Brad Joe Samuel's arrest for non payment of child support. But he keeps dodging the police and no doubt, has help doing so by his family and friends within the police department.

The kids and I have a nice, clean, and beautiful home in which to live. If there is one thing I have learned in life, it is be careful of who you trust. The people that I have trusted most in life are the ones who have betrayed me and my kids the most. I have also learned that often times, family will hurt you more than anyone else in the world. In closing, the kids, Alfred, and I live a very happy life here at the beach.

www.ingramcontent.com/pod-product-compliance
Lightning Source LLC
Chambersburg PA
CBHW051708180726
48283CB00004B/1255